The Wrong Way to Use Healing Magic

vol. 4   KUROKATA

Amako

Usato

Character Introductions

Nea

Aruku

Blurin

He was decked out in imposing,
heavy armor,
and his sword was covered in flame.
He watched me intently
with blank, empty eyes.

"I guess you're not going to let us through, huh Aruku?"

The Wrong Way to Use Healing Magic

Vol. 4

CONTENTS

CHAPTER 1	The Journey Continues!	007
CHAPTER 2	Amako's Premonition!	014
CHAPTER 3	A Village Wrapped in Fear!	046
CHAPTER 4	Attack on the Manor in the Dead of Night!	080
CHAPTER 5	Shock! Trust Betrayed!	110
CHAPTER 6	A Brief Moment of Respite!	146
CHAPTER 7	Healing Magic Versus Fire Magic!	174
Extra	The Start of the Ordeal	208
Side Story	Nack's Road to Llinger	218

Rescue Team Guidelines: Stance on Food

- Eat well, eat regularly, and eat right.
- Maintain a balanced diet.
- Those who do not finish their meals will, without question, be responsible for the dishes.

CHAPTER 1

The Journey Continues!

I had just been to the Wizardry City of Luqvist.

Together with the two heroes—Inukami-senpai and Kazuki—I'd delivered a letter that warned the city of the Demon Lord's forces and requested their support.

It was there that I met a young healer, Nack, who was being bullied by his classmate, Mina. I took it upon myself to build Nack up. I put him through a lighter version of the training I'd gone through with Rose, the leader of the Llinger rescue team. Through hard work and perseverance, Nack prevailed over Mina in a battle that the whole school watched, and once the dust had settled, he made the decision to join the rescue team.

With Nack in high spirits and the City of Luqvist agreeing to support the Llinger Kingdom, I parted ways with Inukami-senpai and Kazuki and headed to Samariarl with Aruku and Amako, where we would deliver our next letter.

I sighed.

It had been three days since we left Luqvist. The journey itself was going smoothly, but I couldn't dispel the anxiety in my heart. The letters in my bag felt like they weighed a ton. Aruku, who was leading our horse a little ways in front of me, turned around at the sound of my sigh.

"Are you worried, Sir Usato?" he asked.

I nodded.

"To be honest, very," I replied.

The letters we were delivering warned of the Demon Lord's attack and requested support. Llinger Kingdom had battled the Demon Lord's forces twice now, and its king entrusted these letters to its two war heroes—Kazuki and Inukami-senpai—and me, a healer with the rescue team. Just a few days ago, we had successfully confirmed the support of the Wizardry City of Luqvist.

"Samariarl, the prayerlands . . ." I muttered.

Samariarl was our next destination, and the first place where I would deliver a letter entirely on my own. This time, I would not have Inukami-senpai or Kazuki's help, and the anxiety I felt was proof of just how important they were to me.

Aruku saw the gloom clouding my features and offered a little encouragement.

"Try not to worry, Sir Usato; you'll have us," he said.

I looked up at Aruku, walking along in front of me. He really was trustworthy.

"There is a limit to what any one person can do on their own," he continued. "However, we can get through almost anything if we work together and help one another."

"You're right. Thanks, Aruku."

It was just the reminder I needed—*I'm not alone.*

I had people around me I could rely on. There was the beastkin, Amako, the knight, Aruku, and my trusty partner, Blurin. Llinger Kingdom had entrusted me with an important task, but being with my friends gave me confidence. Together, we'd find a way out of any trouble.

"But you know, I just *know* I'm still going to be nervous as heck when I have to actually pass the letter over," I said.

I let out another sigh and thought about the letters stored carefully in my backpack. I was, of course, excited to be starting out on a new leg of our journey, but that was drowned out by the sheer responsibility of our task.

Aruku laughed.

"You'll be fine," he said.

"Anybody who knows anything about royal audiences and etiquette is going to see right through me," I moaned.

"Really? From what I've seen, you seem quite good at dealing with people in positions of power."

"I do . . . ?"

"As long as you're well behaved, I honestly think you'll be fine. Nobody's going to expect your manners to be perfect."

I suddenly pictured Rose. I'd lived under her watch for so long that I'd learned to work with people in power . . . which is to say, I'd learned how to handle a very particular kind of wild beast.

"Yeah, I guess Rose *is* a person in a position of power, isn't she?" I admitted.

She was older than me, she was my captain, and she was also my teacher. I looked up to her with a mix of respect and awe.

"So what you're saying is, I'll be fine so long as I talk to people the way I talk to Rose?" I asked.

Aruku thought about this for a moment.

"I think as long as you hold off on the extremely aggressive argumentative stuff, yes."

Oh, so Aruku thinks our conversations are aggressive and argumentative?

Well, he's not entirely wrong, come to think of it.

"Rose, huh?" I muttered

I wondered how she and the rescue team were doing. I knew they'd be hard at work training like always, but what about Felm? Was she used to her new life and the rescue team yet? I thought of all of their mean mugs and the way they'd push Felm around, and it brought a smile to my face.

"Somebody's thinking about something fun," said Amako, stirring me from my thoughts.

"Hm? Fun? Really?"

I wasn't aware I looked that way. Still, it was true that when I thought of Rose, her ruffians, and everyone in the rescue team, I always smiled. The more I thought about it, the more I realized I really liked the place.

"Are you having fun, Amako?" I asked.

"Huh?"

The question felt completely natural to me, but Amako reacted with surprise, and she dropped into a moment of confusion.

Oh no, now I've gone and done it, I thought.

Amako's mother was in a coma, so of course Amako wasn't having fun. I felt suddenly ashamed of even asking her such a thoughtless question.

"I'm sorry," I said. "Forget I said anything."

"But I *am* having fun," replied Amako, her voice just louder than a whisper.

I turned to her, surprised.

"There's Blurin and Aruku and . . . you, Usato. I'm not alone anymore, and that makes me happy. It's fun being with you guys."

She was such a good girl, I couldn't believe it. I couldn't even speak.

She's so pure and innocent, so different from senpai!

From somewhere far, far away, almost like an illusion, I felt like I heard Inukami-senpai's voice.

"What the heck, Usato?"

I shrugged it off. We'd already parted ways in Luqvist, after all.

"Gwah," said Blurin, walking up and slapping my legs.

"Hm? What's up, Blurin?" I asked.

The grizzly growled in response.

I knew it wanted something, but I'd literally just fed it.

"Amako, what does Blurin want?" I asked.

"I think he's probably hungry."

The grizzly roared to indicate that Amako was right.

The bear was such a glutton. I was constantly worried that one day it was going to lay waste to our rations. While I was shaking my head in disbelief, however, an object flew at me, and I caught it.

"An apple?" I asked. "Aruku, is this . . .?"

"We're just starting out on this new leg of our journey," he said, grinning, "so think of it as a morale boost."

He was kind and considerate, and he knew his team well. I smiled back, happy to have discovered this new side to the guy. I gave Blurin the apple, which he quickly and happily chewed up. I sighed at the sight.

"You grumble about it all the time," said Amako, giggling, "but you always go so easy on Blurin."

It was true. I couldn't deny it. I knew I could make things tougher bit by bit as the journey went on, or I could slowly lessen the amount of food Blurin ate. For now, I just wanted to enjoy the ride.

"I sure hope this next part of our delivery goes off without a hitch," I said.

"Indeed," said Aruku.

A journey without any danger and no trouble to speak of. That was what I hoped for. I touched the Omamori that Inukami-senpai gave me before we parted. I prayed that we had a safe trip.

CHAPTER 2

Amako's Premonition!

I hate my magic.
I hate myself for seeing and knowing the future.
I hate whatever god it was that gave me this power.
But I am grateful to that god for one thing and one thing only—that this magic I hate linked my fate with his.

When I woke up, I was standing in the middle of a big room. It was totally creepy. The floor was covered in an expensive carpet, and above me hung a chandelier. I looked around and saw rubble everywhere. Where there were supposed to be windows, there was only a huge hole in the wall, and everything outside of it was pitch black.

I never once thought to ask why I was here. I just knew that I had to remember as much of what was happening as I possibly could.

I saw Usato and Aruku. Aruku looked exhausted. He leaned on his sword for support as he watched Usato. Usato had his back to me. He was talking to someone.

"You're an idiot," he said.

The person he was talking to didn't respond.

"Regret? Why didn't you realize sooner? You already have

everything you wanted, but you ignored your own wishes. You tried to let go of it all."

Who is he talking to?

I couldn't see who it was from where I was standing.

Usato was in bad shape. His rescue team uniform wasn't torn or anything, but it was covered in soot and dirt. A line of blood trailed from his forehead to his jaw. It looked like he'd been through one heck of a fight.

Usato said something, but I didn't catch it; then he moved forward and crouched. For a brief second, I saw the person in front of him. I couldn't see them clearly because of the darkness, but I saw their lips curl as they leaned against the wall, and I saw the fangs they revealed, and then my vision began to waver.

"Usato, watch out!" I cried, trying to jump in front of him.

But at the same time, the person brought out a dagger and moved suddenly toward Usato.

"What?!" cried Usato.

I couldn't see if he'd been stabbed because he still had his back to me, but I saw drops of blood drip to the ground at his feet.

My vision blurred. I reached out as the sight before me grew distant. It was like falling into a slumber from which I could do no more.

I need to know!

What happened to Usato?!
Does he get hurt?
Is he okay?
He survives, doesn't he?
Am I going to be alone again?
I don't want to be alone again . . .

My head spun with thoughts, and my mind filled with terror. This was the way my dreams always were. They ignored me. They showed me what they wanted, and then they ended. They did not show me what happened before, and they did not show me what happened after.

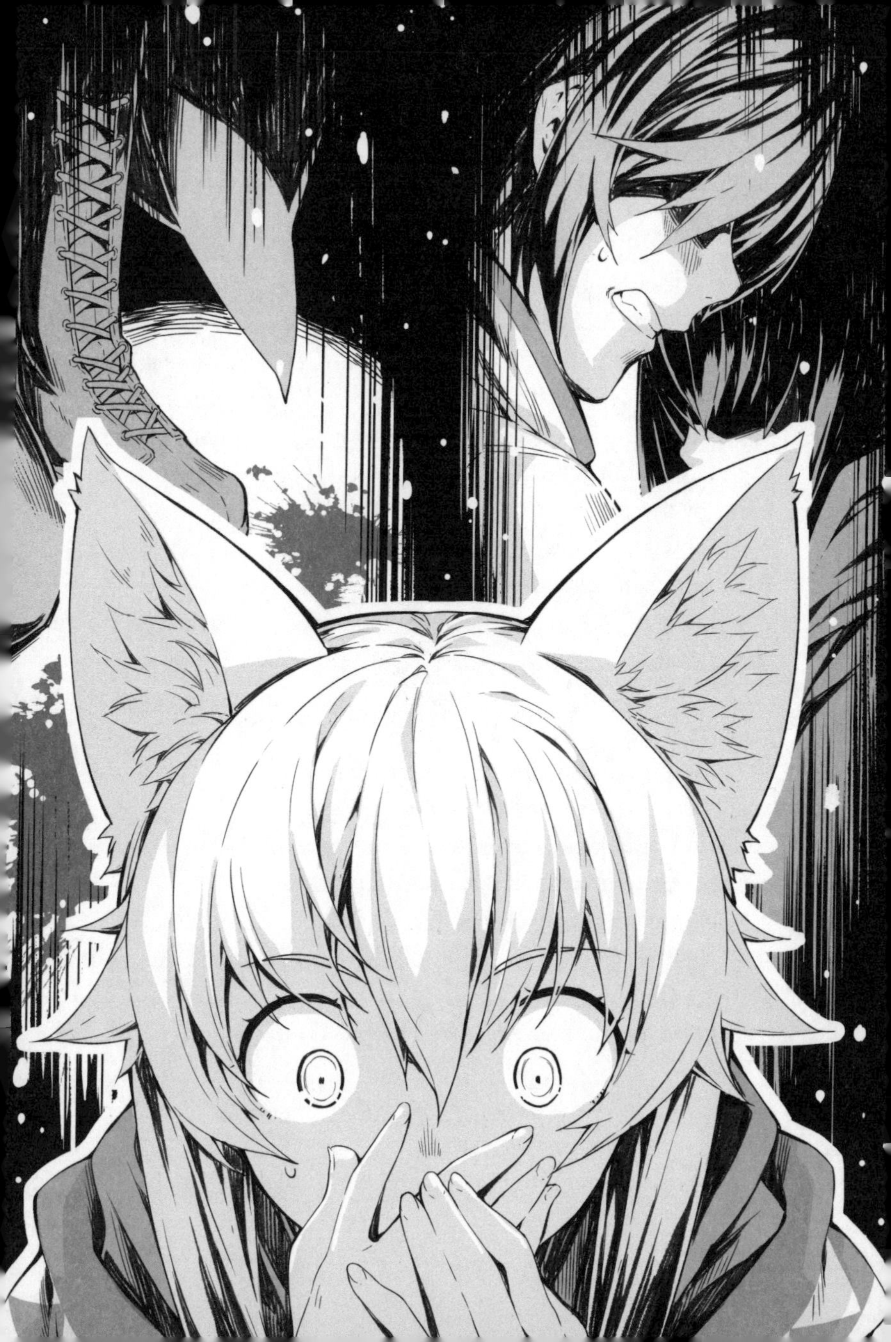

If Usato died, I'd never be able to recover. I never would have thought this if he were just an ordinary healer, but now that I'd traveled with him, I knew—I knew the happiness that came from feeling safe with someone and being able to open your heart to them. I wasn't worried or scared when we were together. I didn't feel any of the painful loneliness I did when I was by myself.

I now knew how wonderful a thing it was to be happy, and I did not want to let the feeling go.

But why? Why had I been shown a future in which Usato was stabbed?

This was why I never wanted my precognitive vision. It was the reason my mother didn't wake up.

But at the same time, it was the reason I met Usato. I was stuck between a present and a future I didn't want to come true, and it was agonizing. I could see it, but I couldn't do anything to change it, and it frustrated me beyond belief.

Did my mother ever feel this way?

I had to face a present I couldn't control and a future I couldn't escape.

It was the absurdity of what we called fate . . .

* * *

"Hm? You dreamed that I got stabbed?" I asked.

"Yes."

It had been one week since we left Luqvist. In the morning, I noticed that Amako wasn't looking well, so I asked her what was wrong. The premonition she shared with us sent a shiver of anxiety through us.

"Uh . . . is it *you* who stabs me?" I asked.

"I'd never do that to you! Anyway, does it ring any bells with you? Know of anyone who might stab you?"

Amako stared at me very, very intently.

"Ring any bells?! How would I know anything about getting stabbed?"

I felt panicked as I ran through the details again.

Amako's premonitions always came true. Unless she interfered with things, there was no changing what she saw. Unfortunately, she couldn't shift the path of the future except in special circumstances, like the time I had stopped the destruction of the Llinger Kingdom.

"And you're sure it's true, Miss Amako?" asked Aruku, leading our horse along.

Amako nodded.

"I don't know exactly when it's going to happen," she replied, "but it will happen in the near future."

"Where does he get stabbed?"

"I don't know. I think in the stomach."

I thought about a knife sliding into my stomach.

"That sounds painful," I muttered.

"Yep," added a dejected Amako.

A silence drifted between us for a moment.

"Wait, that's it?" she asked, bewildered.

"Huh?"

What was so scary about getting stabbed in the stomach? Back at the forests of Llinger, I'd been put through an even more harrowing experience when I fought that giant snake. According to Amako, it was only a dagger, so as long as the knife didn't get me anywhere vital, I could heal myself and strike back.

And if I was being honest, Rose's fists were far more terrifying—and probably more painful—than any dagger.

"No! Wait wait wait wait WAIT!" cried Amako. "What if the dagger is covered in poison?"

"I'll heal it with my magic," I shrugged.

I'd already done that when I fought the snake, so I knew it was possible.

"But you'll bleed . . ."

"How much?"

"A little."

If it was just a little blood, then it probably wasn't so bad. Maybe like a scratch or something.

"So we're all good then," I said.

Amako stared at me.

"Wait a sec," I said. "Quit staring at me like that."

I could read the amazement on her face. *What the heck is wrong with this guy?* it said. I didn't like it at all.

"Sir Usato, it may be best to proceed with caution," said Aruku. "If we think about what Miss Amako has just told us, then we know that in the near future we're going to get pulled into something dangerous."

He was right.

"That's true," I said. "Amako, you can't change that future? You know, like you did back at Llinger?"

Amako shook her head.

Okay, well, that means that one way or another, I'm going to get stabbed.

"Should I start doing more ab workouts?" I asked. "Or is there some way I can knock away the blade before I get stabbed? Wouldn't it be even quicker if I just KOed the stabber before they got the chance? What do you think, Amako?"

"I told you! It's the *future*! It's going to happen! Why are you saying these things?!"

Well, even if it is decided, I still figure it's best to do everything I can to avoid it. That's way better than just doing nothing and regretting that I got stabbed.

"Well, in any case, I'm going to work out. You too, right, Blurin?"

"Grar?!"

"Aha! Just as I thought! Hungry to train, huh?"

I expect nothing less of my trusty partner!

Blurin was so overjoyed about our upcoming training sessions that he slapped me in the legs as we walked.

"Hm . . ." I murmured, looking at Amako.

"Wh-what is it?" she asked.

I'd been thinking about it for a little while now, but Amako was awfully thin. I figured maybe she should work out for the journey ahead.

"Want to join us for training?" I asked. "A bit of muscle might help you out in a pinch."

"Ew, no way."

I didn't think she'd be *that* put off. In fact, she was so against the idea that she even put some distance between us. I was astonished. Blurin, meanwhile, continued to slap my legs. Aruku watched it all happening and laughed.

Though there was an ominous premonition hanging over us, at least our travels were still peaceful for now.

* * *

When evening came, we started a campfire by the side of the road and huddled around it to rest. When it got dark in these parts, you could only rely on the light of the moon. Monsters were more active at night too. To keep ourselves ready in case of any sudden attacks, Aruku and I worked in shifts doing guard duty.

But I wasn't sleepy yet, so I decided to chat with Aruku. Amako was already asleep; her back was against Blurin. He was like a giant blue cushion.

"Aruku, how long until we reach Samariarl?"

Aruku added a branch to the fire.

"We've still got quite a ways to go," he replied.

I knew that it was going to take more than a week, but we still had a long road ahead. There were no cars or bullet trains in this world, so going to distant countries took time, and this brought with it a very particular problem.

"We're running kind of low on food, huh?" I muttered.

"Yes, and we're going to have to do something about that soon."

I nodded as Aruku took out his map and gazed at it. Food was a necessity.

"Well, if worse comes to worst, Blurin and I will hunt some fish or animals," I said.

Blurin growled.

"Don't act like it's the end of the world," I snapped back. "Your appetite is a big part of the reason we're in this mess to begin with."

Aruku chuckled, still looking at his map.

"If that's what it comes to, I'll lend a hand. I'm not a bad hunter, if I do say so myself."

*Wow, he really **can** do almost anything. What a stand-up guy.*

"That said, hm . . ." murmured Aruku.

"What is it?"

"I've heard some weird rumors about the area around the village here."

"Weird rumors?"

And not about the village itself but the area around it?

I was curious, and Aruku looked serious as he answered.

"They say that capable knights, adventurers, and even bandits have suddenly vanished without a trace in the area around the village," he said.

"That doesn't sound weird; that sounds . . . dangerous, no?"

Vanishing without a trace was pretty serious stuff. It was like the rumors people would spread about people being "spirited away" back in my home world. Not unlike being summoned to another world, people could go missing for all sorts of reasons in this world—you could get kidnapped by bandits, attacked by monsters, fall off a cliff . . .

"But they say that some months after it happens—and in some cases, years—the people who vanished come back like nothing happened."

"What? And they're okay?"

And what even happened to them while they were gone?

"All I've heard is rumors and hearsay, but everyone who vanished and came back doesn't have any memories of the time in which they were gone."

"They've lost their memories?"

"Maybe they leaped through time, or maybe someone erased their memories—people have all sorts of hypotheses, but the truth is still unclear."

"When you think about the potential that rare magic is involved, it really could be anything."

"Yes indeed . . ."

Magic existed in this world, and that changed everything. Even the impossible was, to some extent, possible.

And I wasn't so comfortable with these kinds of stories. In fact, I tried to avoid ghosts and horror and all of that kind of stuff. Aruku must have noticed that I'd gone pale because he smiled warmly.

"I think we'll be fine," he said reassuringly. "I haven't heard any rumors in the last couple of years. More than likely, it's just the vivid imaginations of merchants and bandits at play."

"O-Oh, I uh . . . I see."

What a relief. I hope it really is just rumors.

My own imagination had almost gotten the better of me, and I'd started imagining that we'd get lost in a mysterious spiritual kidnapping incident, but if it was just rumors, we were probably all good.

Fantasy worlds didn't need horror. In fact, I didn't want it to even be allowed.

I *really* didn't want to think that ghosts were a thing here . . .

Blurin had been sound asleep, but he let out a short grunt and looked over at the bushes.

"Aruku . . ." I muttered.

"Yep," he replied, noticing the same thing I had.

He picked up the sword at his side. I gestured with my eyes and stood up. Something was lurking in the area where Blurin was staring.

Is it a monster or someone lying in wait?

Whatever it was, it was hiding and watching us, and it didn't seem friendly. We left Blurin to look after the still sleeping Amako while Aruku and I slowly neared the bushes.

As soon as I see them, I'm going to give them one big healing punch.

And if it turns out they're friendly, I'll apologize later.

If it's a monster, we'll just leave it there unconscious.

And if it's a ghost, I'll pick everyone up myself and make a break for it.

I focused my healing magic on my fist and put a hand in the bushes.

"Hoo! Hoot hoot!"

"What the?!"

A black object flew past us from the bushes. I leaned backward in surprise and squinted in the direction the object had just gone. It was a rounded thing with big wings.

"An owl . . .?"

The black owl hooted loudly and disappeared into the

forest. Aruku let his hand fall from the handle of his sword as he watched the owl; then he chuckled.

"I guess we were both a bit on edge after all that talk of disappearances."

"I guess so."

And it was true to say that both of us were pretty tense. We'd have to be a little more relaxed in future.

"But is that what an owl sounds like?" I muttered to myself.

And what was it doing in the bushes, anyway?

I didn't really know anything about owl calls or their habits, but I couldn't shake the odd feeling I had as I stared into the darkness of the forest.

* * *

The following day, we continued our journey. Blurin, Amako, and I all walked ahead while Aruku followed behind us with our horse. It was just another day on the road.

Or at least, that's what I thought.

But then Amako noticed something and put her hand to her ears.

"Miss Amako?" asked Aruku.

"Amako, what's wrong?" I asked.

She'd picked up something thanks to her heightened sense of hearing. I put my hands to my own ears and focused, trying to listen for a voice from afar.

"...lp..."

A girl's voice?

With my human ears, I couldn't make the sounds out properly, but I knew I heard a voice. We all stopped walking. When we listened closely, we heard something from between the trees, followed by a scream.

"Somebody! Help me!"

It was a girl in need of aid!

"Usato!" cried Amako.

"I'm on it," I replied. "Aruku, I'm going to check it out!"

I took off running immediately. I didn't know what was going on, but it was clear from the scream that it was an emergency.

"Be careful!" Amako shouted.

I knew that if I waited for the others, we might be too late. I was the fastest out of all of us, so I would check on things first. At the end of a gentle sloping hill surrounded by trees I saw a number of human figures.

"Who are they?"

I squinted to get a better look. I saw a girl about the same age as me surrounded by a group of men whose clothes were tattered.

"I've got you!" I uttered.

She looked unharmed, but the men around her were closing in, and they looked ready to attack her. To make matters weirder, they were all pale skinned, and their eyes were completely and utterly dead. None of them looked to be in their right minds.

"Get down!" I shouted.

The girl noticed me as I came running, and she did as I told her. I launched a healing bullet at the men hounding her. The force of it sent two of them flying.

"Huh? Wha? They're flying?! Eep!"

The girl's eyes went wide as I stopped at her side, picked her up, and jumped backward.

First things first—I have to make sure she's safe.

"Are you okay?!" I asked. "Are you hurt?!"

"Huh?! Um . . . what did you just . . ."

The girl was amazed as she looked up at me. She had shoulder-length hair and beautiful amber-colored eyes. They were wet, perhaps because she was so scared, and as they settled on my own, I gasped.

Oh my goodness. She's gorgeous. Hm? Is this what they call . . . love at first sight?

"No, wait, that can't be right," I muttered.

I'm not the sort of type to fall in love the moment I lay eyes on someone. Maybe it's because I've been around so many eccentric young women. Maybe now I'm hit harder by the ones who are just normal.

Whatever it was, I pushed the thought aside and lowered the girl to the ground.

"My friends will be here shortly," I said. "I'll handle these guys in the meantime."

"Erm, okay."

That group of men was the main problem at hand. But based on their appearance, they weren't bandits, and they weren't monsters, either. They were all decked out in tattered clothes like homeless people, and their arms swung stiffly by their sides. The eyes that watched me from under their hair were dull and lifeless.

"Why are you trying to attack this girl?" I asked.

The men ignored me completely. Even the men I'd knocked down with my healing bullet were slowly standing to their feet as if nothing had happened.

Guess I better put a little fear into them first . . .

"I don't know why you decided to attack this girl, but . . ." I uttered, shifting my mindset to that of a sadistic, merciless monster.

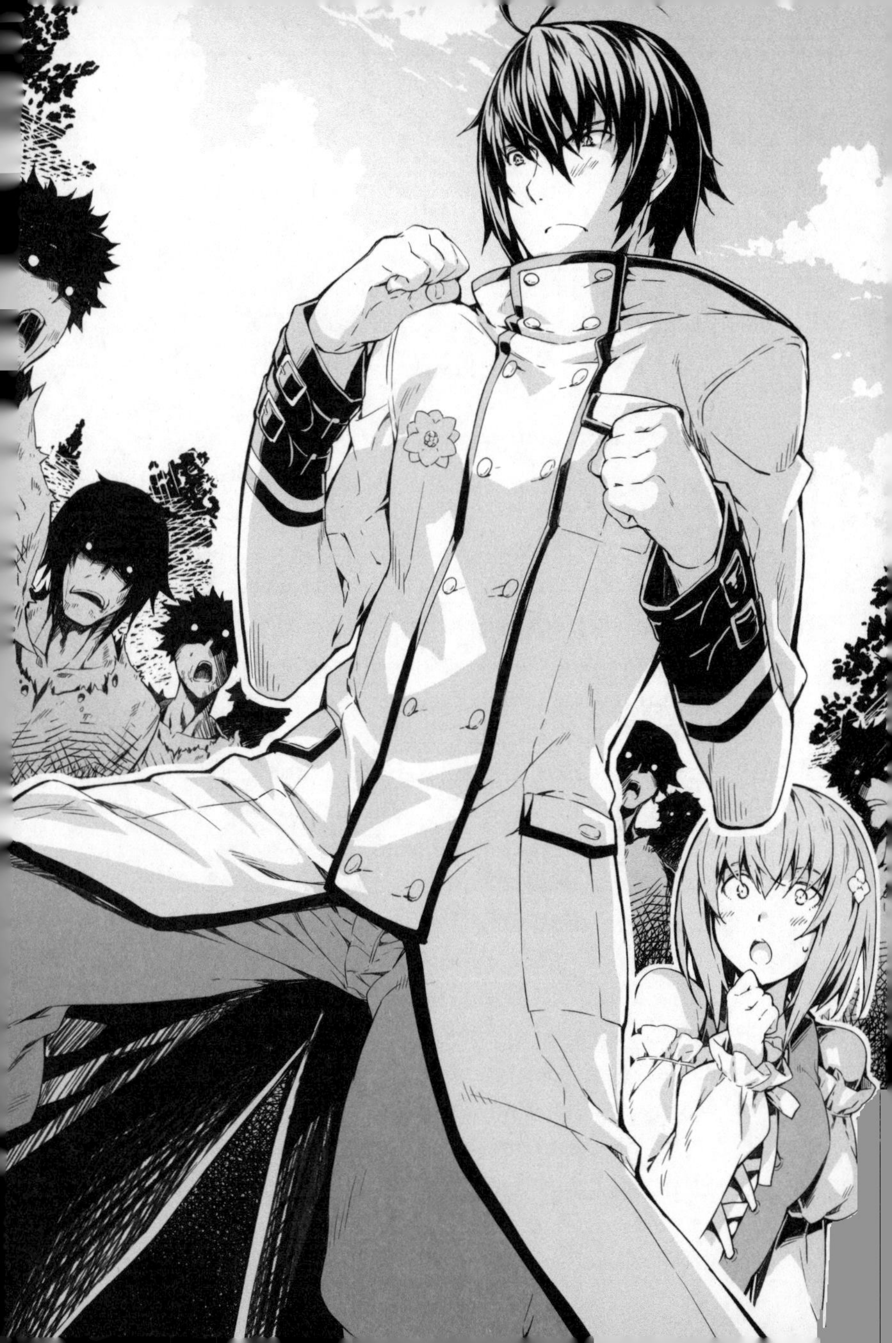

I ran a hand through my hair and let my glare settle on all the men surrounding us.

"Um, these people, they're . . ." uttered the girl.

"Get any closer and I'm tearing your arms off," I said.

"Huh?" said the girl, shocked.

"If you want to keep your limbs then you'll fess up and tell me what you're up to. And if you've got a leader, then you better prepare for the worst, because I am going to show all of you pieces of trash that there really are fates worse than death."

*That sounds about like something Rose would probably say. Then again, she'd probably say something even **more** aggressive.*

"Er, um . . ." muttered the girl.

"Huh? You say somethin' . . .?"

I turned to glance at the girl, but the moment she saw me the color drained from her face, and she shook her head wildly.

"No no no no nope! Not a word! I'm so sorry!"

I guess that gang really put an ungodly fear into her.

But none of them were even the slightest bit intimidated by my threat. They shuffled closer.

"Guess you leave me no choice," I muttered. "Get back!"

I made sure the girl was out of the way; then I silently focused healing magic around my fists. One of the men roared.

"Don't say I didn't warn you!"

As one of the weirdos let out a moan and tried to attack me, I clutched his arm, and slammed him in the guts with a

The Wrong Way To Use Healing Magic 4

healing punch. The man flew some five meters away, his body rolling along the floor until it came to a quiet stop.

I settled back into a fighting stance. I'd held back a little, but I'd hit the guy hard enough to knock him out, I was sure of it.

"How did you even . . .?" the girl uttered.

She was still panicking, but she was taken aback by my first punch. It made me a little sad to think I'd gotten used to the reaction, but I turned my gaze back on the man I'd just punched.

"What was that guy even made of?" I muttered.

Was that guy hiding a steel plate in his shirt? I don't mean to sound rude, but that didn't feel at all like punching a human.

I looked around at the other men as the strange sensation pulsed through my fist. Then, the man I'd sent flying slowly rose to his feet.

I couldn't believe it.

"The hell . . .? How tough *are* you?"

The guy's stomach has caved in?! How?

I hadn't put *that* much power into my punch, and besides, the punch was covered in my healing magic.

Never mind that! How is he even still standing?!

The creepy gang of men let out moans as they tried to attack me in numbers. I responded by slamming each and every one of them with punches, but they were all extremely tough.

"It feels like I'm punching trees!" I muttered.

Does magic not work on these guys at all? Are they some kind of other creature?

I sent another one of the men flying with a punch, but I was nonetheless stupefied.

"My healing punches are completely ineffective?!"

Is my magic of no use here?

But it was true—my magic wasn't working, and I couldn't render any of the attackers unconscious.

I sent another two of the men flying with a spinning kick, then caught one coming from the side and threw him over my shoulder, slamming him hard into the ground.

"What am I supposed to do . . . ?" I muttered.

As I let go of the man I'd just thrown, I formed a healing bullet in my palm and launched it into the face of the man coming up to attack me from behind.

It was a new technique: the blinding heal.

First, I obscured the man's sight with a healing bullet, then slammed him with punches until he flew into a nearby tree. But when the man hit the tree, there was no blood, and no sign of him having been healed by my magic.

"I'm not seeing *any* healing effects on these guys. What does it mean?"

Everyone I hit slowly rose to their feet. It left me perplexed. How were these guys just walking through my healing attacks? Was this the kind of creature they were? Whatever the case, it was creeping me out.

"Who cares?! Just punch them normally! What are you, stupid?!" said Amako, finally making her arrival.

"Well, I mean, I *could*, but . . ."

Just then, another man lurched forward, and I put him down with a hard chop.

"I mean, I'm not super insistent on the healing stuff, but it's worth a try, isn't it?"

I mean, when it came down to it, the healing punch and its variants were a way for me to put my opponents down without hurting them. But I didn't have to be so kind—I could just put them down and be done with it.

"You really went to town on these guys, Sir Usato," said Aruku.

He looked a bit troubled by the situation, but I was glad to see him.

"I didn't have any other choice," I replied.

What I knew from throwing down with them was that they were strong, but they were slow. They weren't demons, but they weren't humans either. They made me think of wild beasts hungry to devour whatever was put in front of them.

"What the heck are these guys anyway?" I asked.

"Their bodies are a mess, and your healing magic has no effect. It's the first time I've ever seen it, but if I had to guess . . ."

They were odd human-like creatures that were impervious to pain and did not bleed. Aruku looked at them for a little longer before saying exactly what it was he thought they were.

"Zombies."

It was the name of a monster that was well known even back in my home world.

"Zombies? For real?"

"They're corpses that can still move, no matter the injury, and while they might be plodding, they wield a strength beyond any ordinary human."

So they weren't really humans at all. They were a type of monster.

I knew a little about the zombies in this world. I'd only ever read about them in books, but zombies were a kind of monster that could be summoned by other monsters. They worked as puppets for the monster that controlled them. But unlike the zombies in my home world, you wouldn't turn into one if you were bitten or scratched.

"So if we've got zombies here, then something is controlling them somewhere nearby, right?" I asked.

"It's very likely," replied Aruku.

Well, at least now I know why my healing magic wasn't working.

Zombie bodies were already dead, and healing magic only worked on the living, so it all made sense. And that meant there was no more need to use it.

"Boy, I sure wish we had Kazuki's light magic at our disposal," said Aruku. "That would work a real treat here, it being holy and everything. However . . ."

Aruku unsheathed his sword and flames crept through the blade as he slashed at the nearest zombie and set it alight. It was fire magic—Aruku had imbued his blade with his fire magic at the same time as he unsheathed it.

That. Was. So. Cool! What do you even call something like that? The most stylish of fire starters?

While I was silently in awe of Aruku's magic, the zombie at the end of his attack let out something akin to a terrified cry as it burned.

"Zombies are weak to fire," explained Aruku. "Leave the rest to me!"

"All yours," I said.

In the face of Aruku's flaming blade, the zombies scattered like baby spiders.

So zombies are weak to fire, huh? Then again, hitting them did feel like punching a dead tree.

"Amako, is the girl okay?"

"Yes," said Amako, her hood up to hide her ears. "She seems unhurt."

The girl then walked past Amako and up to me.

"You rescued me from danger," she said, bowing politely. "Oh, um, I'm Nea! And, erm, thank you!"

"You're . . . welcome . . ."

With the zombies gone, the fear in the air dissipated, and

Nea's smile was blinding in its beauty. She pointed it right at me, and I was so taken that I couldn't even hold her gaze.

I don't know why, but when I looked into Nea's amber eyes, I felt like my heart was being swallowed up.

"So you live in a village nearby?" I asked.

"Yes."

Nea had left her village to gather herbs but found herself encountering a pack of zombies. That was when we found her. She said she wanted to thank us and insisted on taking us to her village.

"Still, I'm shocked . . ." I muttered.

The reason for my surprise was that, for whatever reason, Nea wasn't the slightest bit afraid of Blurin. All of Luqvist's students had been petrified of the grizzly, but Nea showed none of that fear and even smiled at him. Perhaps it was because she had the guts to go exploring around her village—maybe she was braver than I thought.

"You wield an amazing magic, Usato," said Nea.

"Me? What magic?" I asked.

"I've never seen anyone send zombies flying around like that or fire off magic projectiles so fast. Is it a strength-boosting magic? Or are you using wind magic to increase your own speed? Or wait, is it something rare like gravity magic?"

Is this like a long-winded way of trying to say that what I did was beyond human?

The Wrong Way To Use Healing Magic 4

"Heh."

And did Amako just chuckle?

I glared at the beastkin, her shoulders trembling beneath her hood-covered head. I tried to muster a natural smile under the weight of Nea's sparkly, glimmering eyes.

That pure-hearted smile is far too much for one as sullied as I...

"Well, actually, I'm a healer," I admitted.

"Huh? A healer? But isn't healing magic for . . . healing?"

"Yeah. In that fight back there, I wasn't really using any magic. It was mostly just martial arts."

Nea was astonished. She probably never imagined that I used healing magic, which was largely considered useless outside of healing.

"So that means . . . just before . . ."

"That was just fists and feet," said Amako. "It's okay to be surprised. Usato is your stereotypical brainless brawler."

Calm down, Usato. Calm down. You're in front of Nea, after all. You can punish Amako for her big mouth later...

Aruku laughed and said, "Well, one thing Miss Amako is right about is that Usato is unconventional. He's not what you expect. But lots of lives have been saved thanks to his efforts."

Nea snapped back to her senses as Aruku kindly saved my pride. She turned to me apologetically, as if she'd just done something rude.

"I was just surprised!" she said. "I never meant to say you

were stupid or any such thing! I would never!"

Nea was right up in my face, and I struggled to give a calm reply.

"Uh, it's okay," I stammered. "Don't worry about it."

This girl was so different from any girl I'd met until now. She wasn't as outrageously curious as Inukami-senpai, and she wasn't as bright and cheerful as Ururu. If I had to compare her to anything, it would be an abandoned puppy.

"Um, you're a little close, Nea," I said.

I could practically feel her breath on me.

"Ah! I'm sorry!" she cried, backing off as she blushed.

I felt my own face flush in response.

Wait a second. Tell me this isn't what I think it is . . .

"Hmph!"

A moment after her harumph, Amako threw a beautiful side kick right into my shin.

"Wha?! Amako, what was *that* for?!"

Are you going through a rebellious phase or something?

"I can see your future, and a woman is going to take advantage of you. I swear on it."

"WHAT?!"

What was *that* supposed to mean? I wouldn't have cared if it was anyone else saying that, but Amako could actually see the future! Now I would be anxious for the rest of eternity!

"I can't even look at you," she said, "all tongue out and panting like a dog."

"Wait, enough of that, were you talking about a premonition just now?"

Amako said nothing.

"Don't give me the silent treatment, please . . ."

Nea seemed to relax at the sight of us, and she giggled bashfully.

"I think I might have gotten too excited," she said. "It's been so long since I saw anyone who didn't live in our village."

"You mean people don't visit the village?" asked Aruku.

A gloom fell across Nea's face.

"Unfortunately not."

After a short silence, Nea opened up.

"Ever since the zombies appeared, they've been a real headache."

I could see that. I wouldn't want to go anywhere near a village that had those creepy monsters lurking nearby. Merchants probably steered clear, too, which would make daily life more of a struggle. That must have been why an ordinary girl like Nea was out on her own gathering herbs.

"Do you know why the zombies appeared?" I asked.

"No, we don't have the faintest clue."

If we at least knew who was controlling them, we'd be able to come up with a plan to fight back.

"Oh, here we are!" said Nea, pulling me from my thoughts.

I looked ahead and saw the entrance to a village lined with

old houses. It was a bigger place than I had expected. It reminded me a lot of countryside farms back in my home world.

"This is the village where I've spent my whole life, Ieva Village."

Nea looked relieved to finally be back home. I looked around. The village had a simple wooden fence delineating its territory, but it wasn't particularly strong—anybody could have entered if they wanted to.

"Nea!"

The voice came from an elderly woman, who quickly came running over.

"Tetra!"

"I'm so glad you're safe! You left without a word, and I was so worried!"

The old woman wrapped Nea in a hug.

"I'm sorry, but . . . we're running out of herbs," said Nea.

"We're fine for medicine . . . and besides, I was going to have a few of the young men go out gathering anyway. Oh, I'm so glad you're back safe. Who are these people with you?"

"I was attacked by zombies, and these travelers saved me," explained Nea, pulling away from Tetra's embrace to face us. "Everyone, this is Tetra. She's . . . like a mother to me."

Tetra seemed suspicious of us at first, but when she heard that we'd saved Nea, her expression relaxed.

"Thank you so much for rescuing Nea," she said. "She's

got far too much guts for her own good, I tell you . . . I don't know how I can ever thank you enough."

"Te-Tetra!" said Nea, blushing. "Not in front of guests, please! Don't talk about me like that!"

I was curious about their relationship after what Nea said, but they really did seem like a family.

"No thanks necessary," I said. "We just did what anyone would have done."

Did I just say the most stereotypical thing ever?

Either way, I'd kind of always wanted to say it, and I was surprised at how easily it came out.

"In any case, come on into the village. We can talk more there!" said Nea.

"Yes, indeed we can," said Tetra. "Let's see . . . three people, a horse, and a baby-blue grizzly, yes? Well, those two will probably be best in the stables."

We followed Nea and Tetra into the village. There were lots of other villagers there, tending to the fields or looking after horses and cows. They probably weren't used to seeing visitors because we drew a lot of attention.

"You look very tired from your journey. How about spending a night here?" Tetra asked.

"We appreciate the gesture, but we'll be fine, really," said Aruku. "We couldn't burden you like that."

Aruku was right. We had a duty to deliver letters, and we

didn't want to impose on anyone. However, in response to Aruku, Tetra shook her head.

"You must rest when you have the chance to rest," she said. "And you have a child with you, after all. Getting proper rest is essential. Otherwise, you could faint or be exhausted when it's most important. Isn't it best to be in tip-top shape for the journey ahead?"

"Yes, but . . ."

"And besides, it's always best to accept the kindness of the elderly. Who knows how long we've got left!"

The old woman chuckled happily, so Aruku gave up. He smiled, as did Nea.

"Did she call me a child?" muttered Amako. "I'm fourteen."

The beastkin girl was perturbed.

Unfortunately, given her height, it was easy to think she was younger than she was.

"Heh."

"Did you just laugh, Usato?"

"Who, me? No way."

Amako's face flushed red as she pounded on my back. Revenge tasted wonderful.

I will never forget when I have been humiliated . . . most of the time! And when it's time for payback, I'll make you pay . . . if at all possible!

I smiled at how good it felt. Aruku turned to us.

"Sir Usato, Miss Tetra may be right. We're probably tired from all the traveling, so shall we stay here the night?"

"Sounds good to me."

I was used to sleeping on the ground now, but that didn't mean it was very comfortable. And while I felt a little guilty about it, I thought it was fine to accept Tetra and Nea's generosity. Aruku told the old woman as much, and she beamed.

"Great! Well then, let me show you to the stables where the horse and your blue grizzly can sleep."

Finally, a chance to relax. Sometimes it's nice to have people dote on you a little.

The thought felt all the more natural as I looked at the easy smiles on both Tetra and Nea's faces.

CHAPTER 3

A Village Wrapped in Fear!

While Blurin and our horse were taken to the village stables, the rest of us followed Tetra and Nea to their home—a large, wooden two-story house. I was amazed by the sheer size of it, but even more surprised to discover that it was big enough to house even Aruku, Amako, and me in our own separate rooms.

"Admittedly, the place is a little too big for just the two of us," said Nea, mustering a lonely smile.

The three of us relaxed in our rooms until evening, when Nea came and told us that dinner was ready. We all went downstairs to a table easily big enough for six, filled with dishes Nea and Tetra had prepared.

Tetra urged us all to take a seat. She gave Amako a puzzled look.

"Why do you insist on wearing your hood inside, child?" she asked.

I'd been with Amako since the start, so I often forgot that she was a beastkin. But when the realization hit, Aruku and I froze, which only made Tetra and Nea more suspicious.

Amako then began to remove her hood.

"Wait, Amako!" I said, surprised.

Amako shook her head as if to tell me not to worry, then revealed her lustrous golden hair and fox-like ears.

"These two are okay," said Amako. "I see it."

You see it? Like a premonition?

I looked over at our two hosts. Tetra's eyes were a little wide with surprise, and Nea had both hands over her mouth—she was even more surprised than Tetra was. Just as I was about to say something to try and smooth things over, Tetra burst into laughter.

"What a surprise!" she exclaimed. "I never would have thought you were hiding such an adorable little one among you!"

I was so taken aback by the unexpected response that I let out a goofy sounding "Huh?"

"Humans and beastkin are all the same to me," said Tetra. "It's just a matter of ears and tails, really. I'm not so small-minded that I'll denounce others for such things, and besides, I wouldn't be so ungrateful as to criticize the people who just saved my Nea from danger. That said, best keep your ears hidden from the others—they aren't all as open as I am."

Amako nodded. It really seemed like she'd be able to get by at Nea and Tetra's home without having to be on guard all the time.

"I'm so surprised, Amako!" said Nea, staring in awe. "You're a real beastkin!"

Nea didn't bear any ill will. It was clear to everyone that she was just filled with innocent curiosity.

"All the way here, I kept thinking about how you and Usato seemed so close, but now I can see that you two have a really unique relationship. You don't often hear about humans and beastkin traveling together."

"Well, yeah. We know it's not common," I said.

We'd learned at Luqvist just how strange a concept it was to most. But for us, Nea's reaction was even *more* puzzling. I'd never seen demihuman racism up close, so I had no idea to what extent the beastkin were hated by ordinary humans, but I *did* know that Tetra and Nea's reaction to us wasn't common.

"Well, let's save the talk for later and get started, shall we?" said Tetra. "Best eat it before it goes cold!"

"Yes, you're right," said Nea. "Please everyone, help yourselves."

While we were traveling, we'd only eaten fruit and jerky, so warm soup was a real treat.

* * *

We all loved having warm food for dinner. We were served tea afterward.

"The meal was delicious," I said.

Tetra beamed at the compliment.

"I am so glad to hear it," she said. "There's nothing like a homecooked meal, is there? Well then, I'd best get started on washing the dishes."

"Oh, please, let me help . . ." started Nea.

"I won't hear of it. We have guests here, so it's your job to keep them company."

So saying, Tetra left for the kitchen. Left to her own devices, Nea looked a little unsure about what to do next. I wondered if perhaps I should kickstart a new topic of conversation, but before I could, Aruku spoke up.

"I'm just wondering about those zombies from earlier," he said. "When did they start appearing in the area?"

"Huh?"

Nea looked flustered by the question. I was also a little surprised—there was a clear interrogatory tone in his voice. I couldn't help wondering if something about the zombies bothered him.

"Oh, that . . ." said Nea, not sure how to answer.

"Zombies don't come about naturally," said Aruku. "As a monster, they're always raised by someone or something, and they're under that person's control."

Aruku's tone was still serious, and Nea looked anxious.

"Aruku?" I said, but then stopped myself.

I wasn't sure what exactly Aruku wanted to say, but I knew he wasn't the type to be unnecessarily interrogative, either. I decided it was best to see where he was going with this.

"There *is* someone, isn't there?" said Aruku. "I'd wager that everyone at the village knows that someone is up to something."

Nea let out a little whimper.

"Miss Nea," said Aruku. "I understand that you may not want to drag us into the village's affairs, but will you please open up to us about this?"

Now I understood what Aruku was trying to get out of Nea. When I'd first asked her about the zombies, she'd told me she didn't know anything, but that was a lie. The truth was she knew that someone had summoned them. Maybe she even knew where that someone was.

"Hel . . ." said Nea, her voice no louder than a whisper.

She kept her head down, but slowly, she put together a sentence.

"Please . . . help us. Help the village," she said tearfully.

At first, I wasn't sure what to say. I wasn't surprised at the fact that the village had its back against the wall because of zombies, but I wasn't sure if we could take up such a request so easily, either. It was our duty to deliver letters across the lands. Didn't that mean we would have to deny any requests that would slow us down?

"But . . ." I muttered to myself.

As a member of the Llinger rescue team, I wanted nothing more than to help Nea and her village.

"For starters, will you tell us what you know?" asked Aruku.

Nea wiped her eyes and nodded.

"The zombies appeared out of nowhere about two years ago. They came from the graveyard on the outskirts of the village. It was as if all of the buried villagers were zombies all of a sudden."

"And what did they do?"

"They turned the village upside down and injured lots of our people, but then . . . they went somewhere."

Two years ago? That put them at around the time of the Demon Lord's return. I wondered if the two things were connected. Either way, the zombies that had been summoned were all former villagers.

"That's horrible," I muttered.

It was beyond awful to think that the villagers had buried their former family and friends only for someone to use those corpses to terrorize the village.

"Ever since then, the zombies have attacked us and any merchants and travelers walking nearby. Nobody's willing to go anywhere near our village anymore."

"What would make the zombies do that?" Aruku mused.

"I don't know . . . but there's a manor a little ways from the village, and we know that the mastermind behind it all lives there."

Nea looked out the window. It was dark and there was little to be seen out there, but it was likely that she was staring in the direction of the manor.

"Unfortunately, there are zombies around the manor day and night. We can't get anywhere near him."

"Him?"

The zombie summoner is a guy, then?

Nea spoke as if she knew who it was, and she looked at Aruku, Amako, and me before mustering the courage to speak again.

"It's a necromancer. A lord of the dead and a monster that commands and controls corpses. He's made the manor into his home."

"A . . . necromancer?" I asked.

I remembered that it was a monster written about in a book Rose gave me, but I couldn't remember much about them clearly. I knew that they controlled the undead, and . . . they were highly intelligent . . .

I think? Was there anything else about them in that book?

"Hm . . ." I murmured

"Sir Usato, shall I explain?" asked Aruku.

"Yes, please."

I can never seem to find the info when I most need it. I guess I'll fish that book out of my backpack and give it another read.

"A necromancer, also known as a spirit shaman, is a monster extremely similar to a human," said Aruku.

"It's not a demihuman?"

When I thought of "similar to human," I thought of beast-kins and demons.

"Demihumans are flesh and blood creatures like us humans. But monster bodies are formed from magical energy. This is how humans and monsters are differentiated."

"I see."

"Every monster type with a near human form is extremely intelligent. They don't just respond to situations by mere instinct, they consider the circumstances before acting. That makes them noticeably different from your run-of-the-mill monster."

Which would mean that any such monster would potentially be capable of sneaking into a human community unnoticed.

"The necromancer can raise any corpse to work as its servant. This means humans, demihumans, and even wild beasts. They're dangerous because they can take control of any creature that is dead."

"Controlling corpses, huh?" I muttered.

If a dangerous beast like Blurin were to become a zombie, it would be way more than the villagers could handle.

"What's more, necromancers are among the most intelligent of monsters. Those zombies may simply be wandering around randomly for now, but if they're made to work together under the command of the necromancer, we may not be able to hold them off."

"Are they really *that* much of a handful?" I asked.

"Sir Usato, you managed to handle ten on your own, but

even you would struggle against greater numbers."

I didn't want to admit it, but Aruku was probably right. If I had space to run then I could create distance and pick them off, but if I had to take a necromancer on at the same time, I could be cornered and even overwhelmed.

"What a pain . . ." I murmured.

I summarized all the key points in my head. Necromancers were super smart, and they controlled the dead. They looked just like humans and could even pass for humans in human communities. This combination of attributes made them very dangerous monsters.

"Aruku, how strong is a necromancer?" I asked.

"The necromancer itself is not a particularly strong monster. Their strength is in group battles. Zombies are like pieces on a chess board for them—tools for achieving particular goals. Outside of people like yourself, who have powerful physical abilities, taking on zombies isn't easy. I wield fire magic, yes, but my magic reserves aren't infinite—the truth is, we're at a disadvantage in any battle of attrition."

In other words, when I thought of it like the game shogi back home, the necromancer was the king, and the zombies were its foot soldiers. What an annoying foe. We didn't even know how many zombies the necromancer was controlling.

"I wonder what the necromancer wants," I said.

That was the million-dollar question—why did it choose to

attack Ieva Village? If it had already turned the village's dead into zombies, why even bother with the village proper? Even if the goal was to kill off the surviving villagers and make them into zombies, it didn't seem particularly efficient.

"It doesn't make sense," said Aruku. "If it just wants to summon zombies, I don't know why it's so insistent on this village."

"Is it possible it just wants to torment the villagers?"

"It's possible, but necromancers are very intelligent. It seems unlikely that one would go to all this trouble just for a little fun. Perhaps it has some reason of its own for being here."

"I'd much prefer them to just be greedy and on a rampage than to have to deal with something that has motives and a plan," I said.

The most dangerous and troublesome people to deal with were the ones who were strategic about their chaos. The snake in Llinger forest was a good example—it made a show of going completely wild, but it was cool and calculative in its attempts to kill me.

There were all sorts of ways to deal with hoodlums and bandits, but I'd never imagined we'd be looking at having to deal with a necromancer. In a longer battle, we could take out the zombies little by little and then deal with the necromancer last, but that wouldn't be so easy for us, given our limited time.

"Erm . . ." muttered Nea.

"Hm?"

"Er, no. It's fine," she said.

"What is?"

"Our village. Us. You've already saved my life once, and I feel like it's rude of me to ask for your help again. So please, don't think any more of it. We'll be fine."

She spoke each word with a certain sorrow, and I felt my cheeks twitch as I listened.

Like hell I'm just going to leave you all like this . . . You look at me with that kind of despair dripping from your eyes and you expect me to be all like, "Alright then, catch you later!"? The guilt alone would crush me into dust.

Aruku leaned over while I was lost in my own thoughts and whispered.

"Sir Usato," he said.

"Yeah?" I whispered back.

"With something as strong as the Demon Lord around, it's safe to say that anything could happen. Nowhere is completely out of his reach."

"You mean this necromancer might be somehow influenced by the Demon Lord?"

"It's certainly a possibility."

Was the Demon Lord involved in this? If he was, then this was not a problem we could simply ignore.

"That said, *you* have the authority here," said Aruku. "I will follow your orders."

So the decision is mine, then.

Being that Aruku was working as our protection, his logic was sound, but that did not make things any easier. I decided to check with Amako.

"What do you think, Amako?" I asked.

"I'll go along with whatever you decide," she replied. "I think you should do what you think is right."

I felt their eyes on me. I let out a sigh. In front of us was Nea, waiting with worry and uncertainty. I did not think she would begrudge us even if we left her here without doing anything to help. If we put our duties first, we could also avoid confronting a dangerous monster.

I sighed again.

Abandoning Ieva village simply wasn't an option. If I gave up on Nea and her village, I would regret it for the rest of my life. I didn't want to carry that around with me—I'd much rather try and fail than not try anything at all.

"Aruku, physical attacks work on necromancers, yes?" I asked.

"They have a physical form, so yes."

Well, at least that's one thing less to worry about.

I looked Nea in the eyes, then I lifted my hand up to my chest and closed it into a fist.

"If we can knock it out, then we've got a chance," I said. "So let's kick this necromancer into the next dimension and bring peace back to Ieva."

Aruku and Amako nodded.

I didn't like the idea of leaving such a monster to its own devices, especially one that turned the dead into puppets and used them to put a village in danger.

Nea put her hands to her mouth and shook with so much awe that I felt suddenly worried for her.

"Thank you . . . thank you so much . . . I've been so scared . . ."

"Wait. Please. No tears," I said.

Happiness is fine, just no crying, I beg you.

Her voice was shaking, and she had her head in her hands. I didn't have the faintest idea what to say.

"I heard what you were all talking about," said Tetra, entering the room as she dried her hands with a towel.

"Tetra!" exclaimed a teary-eyed Nea.

"I missed some while I was away, but I got the gist of it, anyway," Tetra said as she took a seat next to Nea. "I owe you all thanks. It's not just Nea anymore—it's all of us that you're trying to save. But we cannot leave that task to you alone."

"What do you mean?" I asked.

Tetra smiled.

"I will talk to the village chief tomorrow. I will suggest that we gather our young and healthy to march on the manor and that monster together. After all, it can't hurt to have more help, yes?"

"The more help we have, the better our strategy will work," said Aruku.

Which meant the chances of success rose too. Still, we were dealing with a monster that had protection. Even if the necromancer was physically weak, how would we get around its foot soldiers?

This was not a case of me just punching everything into submission. We would have to work together to bring the necromancer down. But first, we had to get to bed early tonight, so we could rest our bodies and our minds in preparation for what was to come.

* * *

It had been a long time since I'd slept in a soft bed. I woke feeling surprisingly well rested. Amako, too, didn't have to worry about keeping her guard up, so accepting Tetra's kindness turned out to be the right call.

Now that I was feeling in tip-top condition, I left the house at first light.

"So much nature around," I said to myself. "The scenery is so different from last night."

The dark evening sky had given way to a gentle dawn. I let out a deep breath and took it all in. The sunrise was one of a few things that was the same here as it was back in my home world. Here, too, the day started when the sun went up and ended when it went down. Even in a world of magic and monsters, that hadn't changed.

"Well, time for training," I muttered.

I threw myself straight into some warm-up exercises. Ever since we'd begun on our journey, I made sure to train every morning.

Once I was done warming up, I walked over to a nearby tree and looked up at a thick branch about three meters up. I gave the tree trunk a gentle punch to test its strength.

Yep, nice and stable.

I leaped up and grabbed the branch, then lifted myself up, hooked the back of my knees on the branch, then let myself fall back until I was hanging upside down. Then I started doing sit-ups.

After hearing Amako's premonition, I decided I needed to work my abs more, and this was what I came up with. To be honest, I had no idea if the sit-ups were going to be any help at all, but that didn't make them pointless. Even without Amako's premonition, I still had plenty of reason to throw myself into my training.

I let out a breath with each sit up and thought about preparations for our fight against the necromancer in the manor.

I firmly believed that hard work told no lies, and that it always paid off.

For me, that meant training. I always went deeper, faster, and harder—always aiming for the results that came after all the exhaustion and hard work.

"What am I, a workout bro now?" I muttered to myself.

But the truth was I'd become that a long time ago.

I spent thirty or forty minutes doing sit-ups and healing myself without rest. Once my body felt nice and warm, I dropped down to the ground and did some light stretching.

"Getting brighter already," I said as the sun inched farther into the sky, giving me a clearer view of the whole village. "The place looks so peaceful like this . . ."

It was so quiet and so peaceful that it was hard to believe that Ieva had ever been attacked by zombies. Unfortunately, someone had come along to take that peaceful village and plunge its residents into fear.

"Well, may as well keep training."

I took a deep breath to settle my thoughts, then jumped up once again and grabbed the tree branch. Now it was onto one-armed chin-ups. However, before I could get started, I noticed a shadow at the door and dropped back down to the ground.

"Hm?"

Who would be up at this time in the morning?

The person at the door noticed me and timidly came outside.

"Nea?"

"Sorry to bother you . . ."

"No, I'm sorry," I replied. "Did I wake you?"

"Oh, erm, no! I'm always up early, and I noticed you weren't in your room, so . . ."

She smiled awkwardly. I laughed.

"Okay, okay. I see."

So she'd realized I was training and had come to take a look. I got the feeling that, based on her personality, Nea never really knew how to start a conversation.

"Do you always train like this?" Nea asked.

"Yep."

"Um, Usato, are you using your healing magic when you work out?"

"Uh, not quite."

In the beginning, that's exactly what I did, but now things were a bit different. Ever since the battle with the Demon Lord's army, I'd changed up my approach. I was more thoughtful about when I used my healing magic.

"Healing magic heals exhaustion, which is good because you don't get tired," I explained, "but it's inefficient to use it all the time. It makes the training a bit pointless."

"So . . . ?"

"So I train until I hit my limit, and *then* I use my healing magic. I just do that over and over."

I didn't know if it was the best way or the right way to do

things, but I kept doing it because I could feel that I was getting stronger.

"I can't believe that you can use healing magic that way," said Nea. "It's inhuman."

"Huh?"

"Er, nothing."

I feel like I just heard something I shouldn't have heard. Is that who Nea really is? Calm and placid on the outside but harsh on the inside? I'm kind of surprised, honestly.

"Speaking of which, where are you from, Usato?"

"Uh, what?"

I tilted my head in confusion at the sudden question.

"You never told me where you came from," said Nea.

"Oh, *that's* what you mean? Where am I from, huh . . .?"

Oh, you know, just another world. Yeah, that's not going to fly.

Unlike Kiriha and Kyo, who'd become friends I could trust, I didn't think it was wise to tell a girl I'd just met that I'd been summoned from another world. She might not even believe me, anyway.

"I'm from Llinger Kingdom," I said.

"That's so far away . . . but what brings you on this journey? I know you're passing through on your way to Samariarl, but you don't look like merchants."

"Hm . . ." I murmured.

Just how much can I tell her? Well, there's no need to bring up

Amako's mom, that's for sure. Maybe it's enough just to tell her that we're delivering letters warning nations about the threat of the Demon Lord and his army.

I gave Nea a brief rundown of our circumstances.

"Wow," she said in awe once I'd finished. "That doesn't sound like an easy journey."

"Maybe, but we still have to do it," I replied. "If we sit back and do nothing, it could mean the end of the world as we know it."

"The Demon Lord," Nea murmured.

"Have you heard of him here at the village?"

"Yes, I've been told that he's a terrifying force."

Whether you believed in him or not, his presence alone was something that had spread far and wide. And for all I knew, he'd had some kind of influence on the necromancer here. I didn't like the idea, but I had to consider that perhaps an intelligent monster was up to something reckless, and the result of that was what was happening here at Ieva.

"The Demon Lord was defeated by the hero long before I was born," said Nea.

I laughed at how silly her words sounded. I wondered if she was a bit of an airhead.

"Well, yeah, that was hundreds of years ago, so of course it was before you were born."

"Hee hee. Good point."

We shared a smile.

Talking about it made me wonder, though—what kind of a person was the hero who came before Senpai and Kazuki? The stories were like fairy tales and legends now, and it didn't seem like there was any way to know.

"But it's quite scary to think that the demons are going to attack," said Nea.

"But you know what? When you actually meet them, they're not so scary. The one back at the rescue team is your run-of-the-mill competitive meathead."

I thought of Felm, who was being put through the paces back at Llinger Kingdom. Nea reacted to my words with amazement.

"So it's not just beastkin like Amako? You're also acquaintances with a *demon*?"

"Yeah, it just kind of ended up that way. She's not a bad person at heart."

On the battlefield, she was the merciless black knight, but underneath all that armor, she was just another young girl. Well, a young girl with an attitude problem.

"I hope you don't think me rude for saying so, but I can't help thinking that people like you are quite rare, Usato," said Nea.

"Yeah, I'm well aware of that. The moment I was put under the care of the captain—that is to say, my teacher—I've been treated like something of a rare beast."

It made me sad to say the words aloud.

A rare beast, Usato? Really?

"But actually, I'm kind of jealous of you," admitted Nea.

"Jealous? Of me?"

She was jealous of me? A guy who, since arriving in this new world, had spent half of his new life doing backbreaking training?

"Because you've been able to experience so much. In the course of simply living your life, you met rare species like demons and beastkin. In comparison, I . . ."

Nea's voice trailed off, and an emptiness filled her eyes as she stared into the distance.

Wow, things just got kind of heavy.

"I've lived here since the day I was born," said Nea. "I'm so used to this place that I'm sick of it. I know everyone at the village inside and out. So now it's only when we get visitors that I can ever learn something new. Travelers are the only people who can sate my curiosity and quench my thirst for knowledge."

"And Tetra can't teach you anything?"

Tetra looked full of information. But in response to my question, Nea giggled.

"For as long as I can remember, Tetra has looked after me, and she's taught me a lot. But even for her there's a limit."

I figured that was true enough. Even the wisest and most knowledgeable of people could only teach so much. But even aside from that fact, I felt something more persistent in Nea than mere curiosity.

"Knowledge is a treasure that is abundant in this world," said Nea. "I know you have an important duty to see through, but you are allowed a life of freedom beyond a mere village, and that, well . . . that makes me envious."

Whoa, heavy much?! First Nack, now Nea? I'm not a counselor. I'm not a therapist, either. Why do I keep running into people with major life issues?! Is this how young kids in the countryside feel? Kids who long for freedom? But what am I supposed to do about your problems? Healing magic doesn't heal the heart, you know!

Nea must have noticed the look on my face because her eyebrows drooped, and she got suddenly flustered.

"Oh, uh . . . I'm so sorry I brought up something so stupid! None of it is your fault, Usato . . ."

"No, I'm sorry. I could have been a little more sensitive."

Could the situation have gotten any more awkward? I didn't think so.

It was all the necromancer's fault, if you asked me. It was because of the necromancer that nobody was visiting the village anymore. I put all the responsibility building in my heart on that monster's shoulders, then decided to get back to work.

"Well then, I'm going to get back to training," I said.

"Oh, of course. I'll prepare a delicious breakfast for you all!"

"Can't wait."

Nea gave a small, polite bow, then headed back to her house. I watched her go and thought about our talk.

"Knowledge, huh?" I muttered.

Perhaps there was nowhere in the village where people hungry to study could get their fill. For Nea, conversations with travelers and merchants were chances for her to broaden her horizons and learn more about the world.

"And it's not like I can just tell her to go out there and explore . . ."

Nea was no older than I was. It was just plain irresponsible to tell her to get out there and explore a world filled with monsters and bandits.

"So I guess the best I can do is just KO that necromancer."

I jumped up and grabbed hold of the tree branch and got back to my one-armed chin-ups.

* * *

Aruku and I were invited to the village chief's house at around noon. Amako had to hide her ears when she was around the villagers, so she stayed with Nea at Nea's house. All in all, it was Aruku, me, Tetra, the village chief, and five other men.

The village chief had already heard from Tetra that we wanted to take down the necromancer, so we got straight down to business.

However, the village chief was not to be easily convinced.

"I appreciate your valor," he said, looking a little grave as he stroked his beard. "But it's not so easy for me to just let you go out there to fight that monster."

"May I ask why?" asked Aruku.

"Drawing the ire of the necromancer could put our entire village in danger. We may be wiped out completely. I don't even know how strong any of you are."

Ah, so he doesn't want to make matters worse by attacking haphazardly.

"What do you think, Aruku?" I asked.

Aruku nodded to himself and turned to the village chief.

"I am adept at fire magic, which is very effective against zombies. Usato here is so strong that he can brutalize a gang of zombies entirely on his own. In terms of sheer battle power, it's safe to say he surpasses even an experienced mage."

"He can fight zombies . . . ?" asked a villager.

"*And* brutalize them . . . ?" asked another.

Aruku, "brutalize" is going a little too far, wouldn't you say? I mean, you're not wrong, but surely there was a nicer way to put it. Especially when all the villagers are staring at me like that . . .

"Tetra, is what this man says true?" asked the chief.

"I did not see it myself, but Nea did, and she said it was so."

"She's not the type to tell tall tales, either," murmured the village chief. "Well then, how do you intend to fell the necromancer?"

"With a diversionary strategy," replied Aruku.

"A diversion, you say?"

"Indeed. I will act as the decoy and lead the zombies away from the manor so that Usato and another one of our allies can get into the manor undetected. Once there, Usato will hunt down the necromancer and pacify it."

It was a simple strategy, to be sure. Simple and easy to understand.

"Will it really be so easy to get inside the manor?"

"Our friend wields exceptional search and tracking magic. It will not be a problem."

Now I understood Amako's role in the strategy. She'd use her premonition magic to find openings in the security so we could get inside. She was essentially a zombie radar. Then, while the necromancer was focused on its zombies, I'd sneak up on it and smack it in the back of the head to put an end to things.

"What do you think?" asked Aruku. "This strategy has a good chance of success."

The village chief dropped into silence for a moment. Aruku and I waited patiently for his answer.

"We were so powerless," said the village chief, finally breaking the silence. "We had no way to defeat the necromancer, let alone all those zombies. Even if we could handle the zombies, we would only have invited revenge, more zombies, and further injuries to our own people."

"I see," uttered Aruku.

"But on top of that, many of those zombies are our family members. Our friends. It is a horrid thing to have to face them as foes. And more than anything else, I was scared. I was scared that, upon my own death, I would attack those I care for and love—my grandchildren, my son, my wife, my friends, and the village I have tried so hard to protect."

I saw the look of pain on the villagers' faces as the chief spoke. I saw how much it pained them to think that their deaths would only serve to provide more weapons against the village. It was something scarier for them than I ever could have imagined.

"But I am tired of it," said the village chief. "We cannot let that monster do as it pleases any longer. The dead must be given the eternal peace they deserve. Sir Usato, Sir Aruku, please . . . lend us your help."

The chief put his hands on the table and bowed deeply before us.

"We will do so gladly," said Aruku. "But if things get dangerous, I ask only that you all retreat to safety."

It was no easy thing to go into battle against the corpses of those you knew and loved. This necromancer was nothing if not a cruel and heartless sort. It was time to teach that monster a lesson before things got any worse.

Now that we had the village's support, however, there was something I was curious about.

"Aruku, when are we going to make our move on the manor and the zombies? During the day?"

"No, night is better," replied Aruku. "The cover of darkness will make it easier for both you and Miss Amako to move undetected."

Ah, I see. And night will also make it easier to keep Amako's beastkin identity a secret.

Still, a manor in the dead of night was *the* horror movie trope. *And* we knew that a necromancer was roosting there.

I would have been lying if I said I wasn't scared. Nonetheless, we had to do what we had to do.

"In which case, will the attack happen tonight?" asked the village chief.

"Yes," replied Aruku.

The village chief turned to the men behind him.

"Speak to all the men in the village and tell them that we're moving on the necromancer tonight. There's no need to force anybody to do anything they don't want—gather all those with a will to fight. That goes for the five of you, too."

"Understood. But what about you, chief?" asked one of the men.

"As leader of this village, I will be there to oversee the battle."

Understood!" said the men, buoyed by their chief's words. "We'll let everyone know right away!"

The men readied their things and left. Now we had Ieva's full support, which meant all there was left to do was prepare for the night ahead. I looked out the window, ready to fight the necromancer and bring the village peace. Somewhere out there, past all that forestland, was the manor in which the necromancer lived. Defending it was a huge number of zombies, each as strong as they were persistent.

But none of them would be a match for me.

"We're coming for you, necromancer!" I whispered.

Aruku and the villagers would handle the zombies, while Amako and I took on the cowardly necromancer. I ran a hand through my hair and tried to keep cool as the urge to fight swelled within me.

"That expression . . . you truly are ready for anything," uttered the village chief.

"You look like the splitting image of Rose. That's the spirit, Sir Usato!" added Aruku.

But oddly enough, I heard a slight quivering fear in both of their voices. I wondered what they were thinking about.

Ready for anything? Rose's splitting image? That doesn't sound right. Surely I don't look **that** *insanely terrifying . . . do I?*

* * *

While Usato and Aruku went with Tetra to the village chief's house, I waited for them in the living room with Nea at her house. We sat across from one another, both of us looking at our hands so we didn't have to make eye contact. Silence filled the room.

It was *so* awkward.

Nea wasn't someone I'd grown to know and trust like Usato and Aruku. We'd literally only met one day ago. I didn't even know where to start a conversation, and on top of that, I was worried that I'd only be annoying her if I tried. I didn't have much in the way of expressive features anyway, so I had a feeling that maybe Nea didn't have a good impression of me.

"Why are you traveling together with Usato, Amako?" asked Nea casually.

She put a cup of tea in front of me on the table between us.

"Huh?"

I wasn't sure what to say.

"What's wrong?"

"Oh, uh, erm . . . you want to know why I'm traveling with Usato?" I sputtered, panicking to answer.

Nea responded to my panic with her own.

"Oh, I don't mean to ask because you're a beastkin, if that's what you're thinking?!" said Nea, waving her hand. "It's just that you're so young, and I was curious as to how you and Usato ended up traveling together."

"Young," I said with some disdain before pulling myself together. "Huh, okay, whatever."

I'm fourteen. Fourteen isn't young. I'm not a kid.

I thought about why I was traveling with Usato. The first reason was because he'd promised to help my mother. My mother was asleep in my homeland, the Beastlands. I loved her, and I wanted to save her.

I wanted to see her again, awake this time, and I wanted to hug her.

It was those feelings that pushed me to leave the Beastlands and eventually arrive at the Llinger Kingdom. There, I felt that *I* was saved by all the kindness I experienced. Llinger was a place where people were kind to one another. None of them discriminated against other races.

But even then, I couldn't give up on my mother, and so I continued to search for healers. I found three of them in the Llinger Kingdom. All of them were vastly different in terms of personality. They were also vastly different from the healers I'd learned of in other nations—there was a warmth and generosity to them. However, I knew that none of them would come with me to the Beastlands to save my mother.

Just as I was about to give up, I saw a premonition—I saw the Llinger Kingdom fall to an attack from the Demon Lord's forces. When it hit me, the life drained out of me. The people who had accepted me, the town, the whole nation—I saw it all engulfed in flames.

Everything I did would have been in vain. I was filled with fear.

I have to run, I thought. *I don't want to die.*

But still, I could not let go of hope.

Before knowing what kind of place Llinger Kingdom was, I would have been all too happy to abandon it. But now I *did* know, so I searched for anything that might save us.

And my search brought me to him—the young man who would protect those I cared about and save them. The first time I saw him in town was the first day I ever believed in destiny.

"There is someone very close to me I want to save," I said. "And people I want to be with. That's why."

"People to be with . . ."

Traveling with Usato was fun. It was so much fun that when I talked to him, I forgot that I was a beastkin.

"I'm scared of being alone," I said. "I don't want to be alone ever again. Now that I've felt true kindness, I feel like I'm not as strong as I used to be."

When I left the Beastlands, I used my premonition magic to do whatever I had to—I snuck into countries, I stole food to survive, and I got by while looking for some way to save my mother.

"I know how that feels," said Nea, nodding. "I was alone too. But thanks to the people around me, I've made it to where I am today. But your fear of being alone? I don't think that's a weakness."

"You don't?"

"Humans, beastkin, monsters—nobody can live without support. We can put on a front and try to get things done all on our own, but at some point we break. When that happens, you can't recover by yourself. Maybe this isn't the nicest way to put it, but life itself is terribly fragile—unless it has something to cling to, it falls apart."

I know this is coming from me, but Nea is **way** *more philosophical than she looks. I'm actually amazed.*

Nea noticed the surprise on my face, and she blushed.

"W-well, that's what Tetra told me, anyway," she said.

"Is that so?"

Why the strange reaction just now?

"O-oh, by the way, does Usato always get up so early to train?"

"Yeah, he's crazy about training."

I'd already heard from Usato that Nea saw him training in the morning. Anyone who witnessed it themselves thought it was otherworldly. It looked ordinary at first, but the length, the amount, and the pace of it—all of it made people tilt their heads in disbelief until they actually, literally, couldn't believe it.

"I don't mean to sound rude, but is Usato *really* a healer? Are you sure he's not actually some kind of other magic type? Like, is there some kind of special power inside of his body?"

"Nope. He's a healer, through and through. Probably."

"What do you mean, probably?!"

It was only natural that Nea was dubious, but there was no doubt about it—Usato was a healer. And just as with all healers, all he could do was heal. He couldn't use any of the general magics available to other magic types.

Recovery magic was one such spell within the range of general magic, and so there was a tendency for people to see it as better than actual healing magic because anybody could use it.

"I'm just so curious," muttered Nea. "How in the world did he get to be so freakishly strong?"

"You're interested in magic?"

"Yes. I can't use any myself, but I want to learn more about it."

"How very studious of you."

The secret to Usato's strength . . . was *what*, exactly? His unbreakable will? The result of endless training? Both answers were right, but both were also a little off the mark.

"I don't know," I said.

"Oh. I see."

"Try not to think about it. I don't think you'll ever get an answer by thinking about it logically."

Nea giggled.

"You make it sound like he's completely illogical."

Weird. The moment I heard her words, I thought of Usato as an illogical monster.

I couldn't deny it even if I wanted to.

Nea's eyes grew wide as she read the message in my silence.

"Well, he's not *quite* that nonsensical," I said.

"I couldn't believe that he could overwhelm those zombies with just his physical strength alone."

"Hang out with Usato long enough, and that kind of thing stops being a surprise real quick."

Nea put a hand to her mouth and chuckled. I couldn't help but giggle along with her as I reached for my cup of tea. But as I looked down, I heard something.

"I'm so jealous. So very, very jealous," Nea whispered.

"Hm?"

I never would have heard it without my beastkin ears, but I heard Nea's words loud and clear.

"Is something wrong?" she asked. "Is the tea not to your liking?"

"Uh, no, it's nothing. The tea is delicious, thank you."

"I'm glad."

It had to have been an illusion or a trick. I didn't want to believe that in the midst of our pleasant conversation, Nea's eyes had, for the briefest of moments, turned to an icy cold gaze.

CHAPTER 4

Attack on the Manor in the Dead of Night!

When the sun set, the village outskirts were wrapped in darkness. With the clouds covering the moon, the only light was coming from the Ieva village houses. In the night, the light of the moon was all you could rely on, and so usually there was a gloom in the air, but tonight things were different.

Tonight, the darkness was perfect for necromancer hunting.

"I never imagined that so many people would come out to help," said Aruku.

We were waiting at the entrance of the village for the village chief, who now arrived with at least thirty people in tow, all of them ready to help in our attempt to take down the necromancer.

"This situation has vexed us all," said the chief, "but none of us had the courage to face the necromancer alone. We have rediscovered the will to fight, and we owe it all to you."

His words both encouraged and embarrassed me. But even with the villagers helping us out, I knew that I had to be prepared. If I failed to defeat the necromancer, it would likely turn its rage on the village and its inhabitants. If *that* happened, then I'd have no other choice—as much as it would pain me to do so, I'd crush the zombies' limbs and render them incapable of any movement whatsoever. I had to prioritize the safety of the villagers.

"Chief, I didn't mention it earlier, but I'm good at first aid magic," I said. "So even if it's after the necromancer has been defeated, please bring me any injured people and I'll heal them back to full health."

If I told them I was a healer, it might make the villagers worried, so I made it sound like I was good at general magic.

"Sir Usato, you have our thanks," replied the chief.

He looked relieved. It must have been nice to know that the injured could be helped during and after the battle. When he saw that the chief and I had finished talking, Aruku politely got his attention. It was time to explain to everyone how the strategy was going to work. Aruku was a knight. He knew the ins and outs of battling in formation, which was a confidence booster for everyone. I looked out at the crowd of villagers as Amako peeked up at me from under her hood.

"Usato, are you bringing Blurin?" she asked.

"I left him at the stables. He knows that if he were out here, he'd frighten the villagers. But anyway, how's your magic? Feeling okay? I'm going to be relying on you for a lot of this."

"I feel great. And I can also see well in the dark, so leave dark locations to me."

"That's great. I'll totally ask for your help."

Even though I was used to the Llinger forest, that didn't

mean I could navigate the darkness of *this* forest without getting lost. Amako's beastkin eyesight would be a huge advantage.

"It's the first time we're fighting together."

"Yep, after all this time, here we are."

We'd traveled together a lot, but this was the first time that Amako and I would be working together to complete a specific task. And because we'd have to make full use of Amako's premonition magic for this particular covert operation, everything came down to our ability to work as a team.

"I have a feeling we're going to do great," I said.

Amako paused for a moment before replying.

"Yeah . . ."

"Huh?"

Was she nervous or something? Usually, she would reply with something like, *"Are you okay, Usato? You're being so honest it's creepy."* But instead, she simply agreed. I felt a little embarrassed, and for a moment, I wasn't sure what to say.

So, I decided to break the tension with a joke.

"Well, from what I hear, necromancers aren't particularly strong, so we shouldn't have any issues, but if we do . . ."

"If we do, then what?"

"Then I'll carry you on my back."

"Huh?"

I had never heard Amako sound so cold before. I held a finger up while I waved a hand to tell her that she had the wrong idea and explained why.

"You read the enemies' movements and I knock them down. Yeah, it's a simple strategy, but with you on my back, we're an unstoppable combo."

Amako said nothing.

I continued. "If you have to move around while you're focusing on your premonitions, you'll only be able to glimpse short instances in time. So, you can let me handle the moving by piggybacking you. That way, you can just give me directions—how the enemy is going to move, what they're going to do, and how they're going to do it."

Still, Amako said nothing.

"With my reflexes and your foresight, we'll read the enemy before they have a chance to move and hit them with the best shots we've got. Basically, what I'm saying is—like I said before—we're unstoppable together."

Amako simply stared at me. I couldn't bear her expressionless gaze. She was watching me from within her hood. I felt the strong urge to apologize. The light glimmering in her eyes was just too overwhelming.

"I'm sorry," I muttered.

"Usato!"

Just then, an unexpected voice shouted from behind me.

"Hm?" I murmured.

I turned to look at the voice, and I saw Nea running toward me. The area was lit up by the nearby houses and the torches that people carried, but it was still quite dark. She ran over cautiously and held her breath for a brief moment.

"Usato!" she cried.

"Whoa!" I said as she suddenly hugged me.

I never imagined that she would ever do that, and after a brief moment of complete and utter panic, I attempted to calm myself and looked for help. However, Aruku, the village chief, and the thirty-something villagers with them simply watched us and grinned. The younger villagers, however, all shot angry glares in my general direction.

Never in my wildest dreams did I ever think anyone would be jealous of me in this world.

"Hey, Usato, what are you doing? Hm? What's going on?"

It was Amako, looking up at me with that same expressionless gaze.

Please, at least give me the chance to explain that I'm not doing this of my own volition!

"Usato, I . . . I'm just so worried about you!" said Nea.

This isn't my role in these kinds of situations. It's Kazuki's!

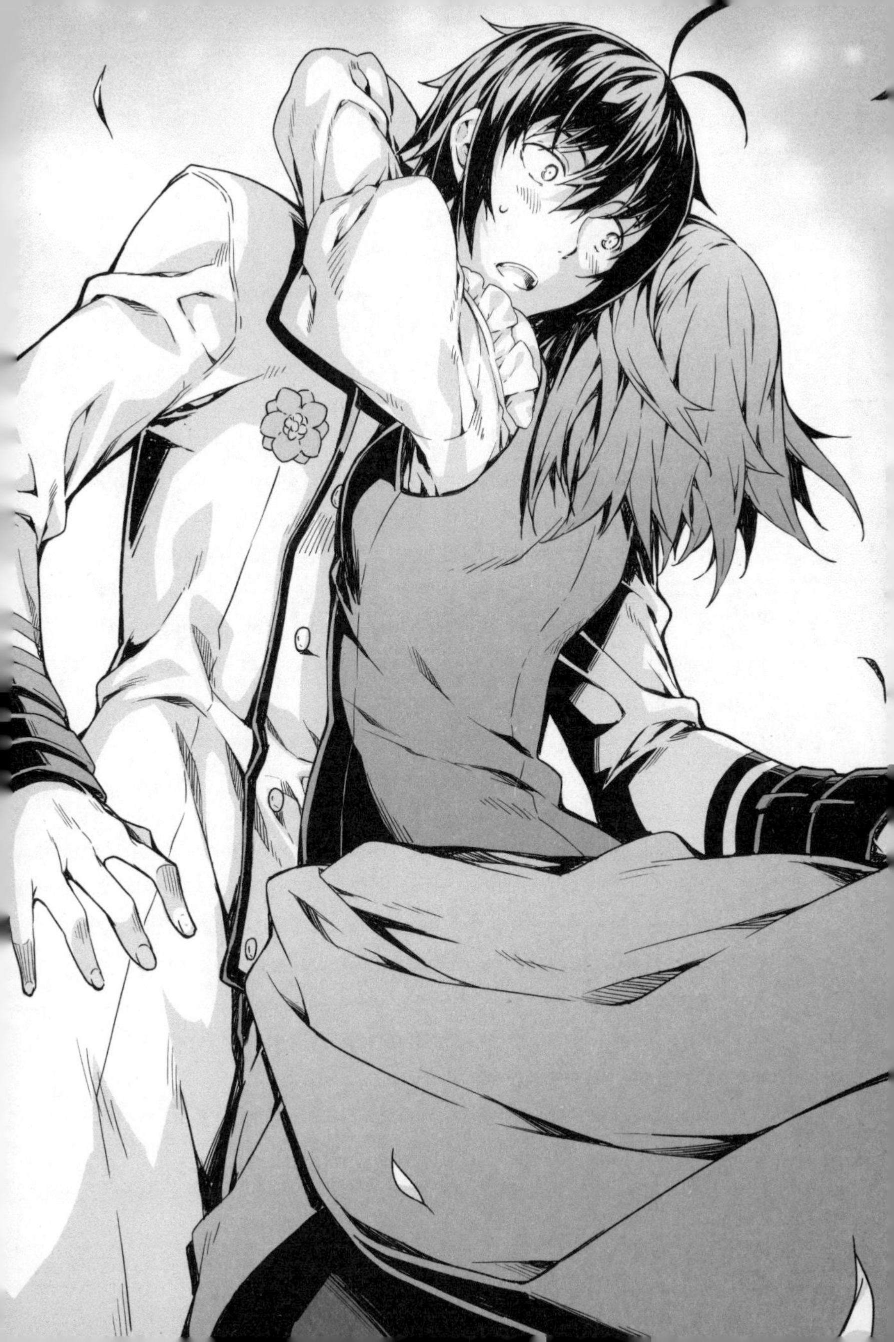

I had no idea what was going on, and it was all so sudden that I could barely feel any of it.

Why is Nea hugging me like this so suddenly?

I couldn't just pass it off as a kind of suspension bridge effect, the fear bringing out excessive and misdirected emotions in her. Given the circumstances, there just hadn't been enough time for that. And even if it *was* a kind of love at first sight, clearly Nea was confused. She'd only met me yesterday.

"Nea," I said.

My voice trembled, but I took her by the shoulders and gently pushed her away. I looked into her amber-colored, teary eyes. I felt my heart begin to waver. I did my utmost not to let myself get swept away in the moment as I spoke.

"You don't have to worry," I said. "I'll be fine."

"Huh?" Nea said.

Her eyes went wide with confusion, but I ignored it and went on.

"I am going to find the necromancer terrorizing this village, and I am going to smack it until it stops. So you just wait here and stay safe."

"Oh, thank you. You're really going out of your way to protect all of us," she uttered.

Nea still seemed very confused by the words I'd spoken, but she nodded her head and left.

I let out a sigh. I just knew that if Inukami-senpai had been here to see that, it totally would have erupted into a scene. And yet, at the same time, I couldn't help but feel a certain regret about pushing Nea away. I'd been punched and kicked and verbally abused by one particular woman, but I'd never been held in a way that was so gentle. Still, I knew that if I thought about Rose's rough and ready treatment too much longer, I'd be brought to tears.

"Aruku, shall we head off?" I said.

"Yes. Everyone, are you ready?"

The villagers raised their torches and replied as one. Everyone was ready, and all that was left now was to bring down that nasty necromancer.

* * *

As we walked along the road, we didn't encounter any zombies. It was so strange. Were they all concentrated around the manor? Or had they been separated and were now roaming free away from where we were? Whatever the case, we managed to get to a position where the manor was in sight without anyone in our group getting injured.

"So that's the necromancer's manor," said Aruku, as we looked at the dim shape of the building in the distance.

It was dark. The whole building wafted with an aura of gloom.

"Usato, there are zombies around the manor," said Amako.

"How many?"

"More than I can count."

I nodded and frowned. I couldn't see them clearly, but Amako was right—there were dark shapes wandering around the manor grounds. There were enough of them that a full-frontal attack on the manor was just folly. Torch in hand, Aruku stood in place and surveyed the situation.

"Sir Usato," he said. "Let's split up here. I'll head to the front of the manor and draw the zombies away, just like we planned. You and Amako try getting in from the other side."

"Got it."

I looked over at Amako. She was ready to get moving. I could see by the confidence in her eyes that she was mentally prepared.

"Let's do it, Amako," I said.

"Okay."

"Be careful, Sir Usato," said Aruku.

"You too, and everyone else. Please don't do anything rash."

Amako and I watched as Aruku and the villagers headed off, then we left the main path and took to the darkness of the forest. It was *very* dark, and I had to be careful not to make too much noise.

"Amako, take the lead," I said.

"Okay, stay close."

Amako took off her hood and walked close behind. I clenched my fists in case we ran into any zombies.

"Usato, stop," whispered Amako.

We ducked down, and a few seconds later, we heard something lumbering through the bushes. A zombie passed by, moaning as it went.

"If you weren't here, that would have found me for sure," I said.

Those premonitions sure were something. They were almost too convenient. I made a mental note not to rely on them too much.

Just then, from over near the manor, we heard the roar of men. We looked over to see Aruku and the villagers, illuminated by torchlight, not far from the manor entrance. All the zombies around swiveled their heads to the sound, and were drawn like moths to the flame, shuffling their feet as they headed toward the villagers.

"They've started the diversion," said Amako.

"So far, so good," I added. "Now it's up to us."

"Yep. Let's do this."

I took a breath, then started moving again. We circled to the back of the manor. When we were sure there were no zombies around, we left the forest and ran for one of the manor windows. I put a hand to the window and silently lifted it up—it opened without issue.

"The windows aren't locked," I whispered.

I know it was a monster we were talking about, but I felt they were a bit careless. There was a chance there were traps waiting for us, but we'd come too far to pull out now, so Amako and I crawled inside.

The room we entered was unusually well kept. That was somehow even creepier. We tiptoed to the door, and I glanced at Amako to let her know I needed her premonition magic. She nodded and looked at the door as though she were staring straight through it.

"There's nothing on the other side," she said. "The door exits to a corridor. On the right, and at the corner . . . I've got one."

A zombie was waiting around the corner.

"Alright, then let's take care of the zombie and make sure it can't do anything. Before that, though . . ."

I walked over to the window and pulled down a dusty curtain.

"Amako, tell me when to go."

"Leave it to me."

We opened the door, silently walked down the corridor, and neared the corner. Then I waited for Amako's signal.

"Usato, now!" she hissed.

I leaped out and my eyes met with a zombie's. I didn't hold back. I launched two punches as hard as I could on its arms. The zombie's arms went flying. The force of the blows sent the zombie stumbling backward. Still, I couldn't let it hit the wall because it would make too much noise, so I stomped down hard with my right foot on the zombie's left. Without a moment's hesitation, I followed up with a sweep, breaking the zombie's knees and folding its legs in two. To finish things off, I wrapped the curtain around its mouth to keep it quiet.

"A job well done," I said.

At my feet, the essentially limbless zombie rolled around, attempting to moan through its muffled face.

"Eww," said Amako, her face was going pale. "I didn't even see it. One minute there's a zombie, then all of a sudden, he's got no arms. Then all of a sudden, his legs are broken and he's rolling on the floor. I figured you weren't going to hold back, but this . . ."

"Just what do you think I am, Amako?" I said, chuckling. "I'm not a monster, you know."

"I can tell you're faking that laugh, Usato."

Her lips twisted into a cringe as I hefted the zombie onto my shoulder. Yes, I was merciless in my attack, and I didn't hold back, and if I wanted to, I could do the same thing to a living, breathing human. But I didn't think I would ever hit a human with everything I had—well, as long as I didn't forget myself, or *want* to kill my opponent.

"Let's hurry," I said.

I put the zombie in a nearby room, and we got back to our search. I could still feel the sensation of punching that zombie in my knuckles. It was heavy. The feeling was only heavier now that I knew these zombies had committed no crimes. They were once simply villagers here. I felt like I was about to be crushed under the weight of the feeling. I clenched my fist.

"Damn it," I muttered. "I can't stand fighting."

The manor was quite a spacious place. It had so little in the way of security that I was bewildered. Outside of the one zombie we'd encountered, we didn't find any others wandering around. I wondered if the place had been entirely empty right from the start. But based on how nice the place was, I knew that *someone* had to be keeping it clean.

"Whoever lives here has a real thing for antiques, huh?" I muttered.

We passed down a corridor filled with suits of armor, neatly standing in rows. I knocked on one of them with a hand to check the metal. I wouldn't have thought anything of it if all the armor was the same, but each set was different. They were all different designs, and they all held different weapons, like swords and morning stars. One huge set of armor, in particular, stood out because of its weapon.

"What is this, a spear?" I muttered. "No, wait, it's a halberd. It's huge, though. No ordinary human could handle something like this."

It was a spear that stood taller than I was, with a huge axe blade at the end of it. The suit of armor carrying it was at least two meters tall, too, but they seemed totally mismatched.

"This place is like a museum," I said.

We walked the corridor as I thought pointless thoughts, and then Amako spoke.

"But I don't think these are very old," she said. "I've seen this armor on my travels."

Which meant they weren't antiques. This raised another question: what was relatively new armor doing in a place like this? Were all these different sets of armor here because the owner of the manor was interested in armor?

"Is it possible that this has something to do with that rumor that Aruku was talking about?" I wondered aloud.

He told me that people had gone missing suddenly, but it hadn't happened in quite a few years. Was everything we were looking at now somehow connected to the stories of the knights, warriors, and bandits who went missing? That would mean that the was the culprit. But if that were true, one thing didn't make sense.

"Why didn't Nea or any of the villagers tell us about that?"

This was suspicious, of course, if we assumed that the villagers themselves had heard the rumors. But if people had gone missing around these parts some years ago, the villagers surely would have suspected the necromancer of having some role in it. And yet, none of them said a thing.

While I was lost in thought, Amako stopped in place.

"Wait," she said.

"What is it?"

Did she find something?

"There's a room up ahead with the lights on."

"Really?"

Was it time? Was it time to confront the necromancer?

We proceeded forward cautiously, and I noticed light leaking from a door up ahead.

"Is the necromancer in there?" I asked.

"No."

Amako had seen past the door, and she looked puzzled. Had the necromancer noticed us? Amako used her magic one more time, then opened the double doors into the room.

"What the . . .?"

The room was like a library, filled with books piled as high as the ceiling. I couldn't believe how many of them there were.

"What is this?" I asked as we stepped inside. "A study?"

"How long would it take to read all of these books?"

"An unbelievably long time."

I walked to a table, which had some magical tools on it, and noticed a book. The book was brown and old and falling apart. I picked it up, turned it over, and looked at the title.

"*Record of the Hero*? What is this book?" I uttered.

The author's name was no longer readable, but it seemed like the book was about the hero.

"So, it's not a book so much as it is a diary?"

This wasn't about Kazuki or senpai, though—this was about the hero who came before.

Filled with curiosity, I opened the book. I turned the old pages carefully, fearful that they might crumble, and found that most of the pages were so badly weather worn that the writing was no longer legible.

"I can barely read any of this. Well, I'm certainly not going to be able to read anything just skimming it."

Just as I was about to close the book, a line jumped out at me. In the center of the page was a line written in big script.

He hated humans. He loved us.

By "he" they meant the hero, right?

Did that mean that the hero loved some other species that was not human?

I didn't actually know if what was written in the diary was true, but I was nevertheless intrigued.

"Guess I'll take it with me," I said.

I put the diary in my chest pocket, and admittedly, I felt a little guilty about it. It being theft and all. But then I noticed a black book near where the diary had been.

"Hm? What's this?" I muttered, opening it up. "Huh? I can't read any of it. How odd."

The text was completely foreign to me. I could understand most texts here in this world, but not what was written in this particular book.

"I don't understand . . ." I muttered.

When we'd been summoned to this world, a spell had been cast upon Kazuki, senpai, and I that let us understand languages. Just to make sure it wasn't me, I grabbed another book for comparison and confirmed what I thought: I could read it. The black book was clearly unique.

"Amako, can you read this?" I asked.

"Hm? What is it?"

Amako had been idly poking around at books elsewhere. I passed her the black book. As soon as she saw it, her eyes went wide.

"No way . . ." she uttered.

Her response sent warning bells ringing in my head.

"What's up?" I asked.

With a slight tremble in her voice, Amako explained.

"This is . . . a book of sorcery."

I wasn't sure what she meant. I wasn't particularly familiar with the word, so without thinking, I repeated it straight back to her.

"Sorcery? Wait, so you can read what's in the book?"

"No, but that's how I know that this is a book of sorcery. I saw one once back home in the Beastlands. It was the same as this. Usato, you're not supposed to be able to read this."

"You mean it's better that we can't?"

But wouldn't that mean that nobody could understand it? Amako looked frustrated by my puzzled expression.

"Usato, this is really bad," she said, still clutching the book. "This means that the necromancer might also be capable of sorcery!"

"And that's . . . not good?"

"It's *so* not good."

Clearly, Amako saw this as a major crisis. Her panicked expression told me exactly how dire the situation potentially was. Sorcery was a word that, in my home world, brought to mind dark and wicked imagery. It seemed like sorcery was something slightly different here.

"Okay, well how about you start by explaining to me exactly what sorcery is?" I said.

The question calmed Amako down a little. She took a deep breath, looked me in the eyes, and nodded.

"Like magic, sorcery is activated by magic power."

"So the energy source is the same, then?"

"Yes, but aside from that, they're completely different. Anyone can use magic once they know how it works, but sorcery is recorded in books. You can't use hex formulas unless you decipher them first."

Hex formulas? Is that what these indecipherable words are?

"Is it even possible to understand this?" I asked, pointing at the book. "All of it looks like complete gibberish to me."

"Of course, it does. Hex formulas are not simple things that are remembered in just a day or two. Learning to use them can take as long as fifty years."

"Fifty years?!"

What the heck?! You'd be a grandpa by the time you learned **anything**. *And if she said "at least", that means some books take even longer to understand.*

"That's sorcery," said Amako. "It's made up of skills that people spend their lives learning to master."

"Who would even come up with something so strange though?"

"Well, whoever it was, I don't think they were human."

That much was obvious—whoever came up with this sorcery didn't even consider human lifespans.

"But is it worth spending so much time to learn sorcery?" I asked.

"Not usually, but it can definitely make you more powerful. One of sorcery's few strengths is that you can learn to use it regardless of what magic you were born with."

"But the price for that seems way too high."

I was pretty certain that any human who tried to learn sorcery was probably insane.

"But it's not all bad," said Amako. "Unlike magic, sorcery is powerful in very specific areas."

"What do you mean?"

"Magic changes based on how it is used, but sorcery is very specific and very powerful within its limited area of use. I've heard that some sorcery even tampers with time, space, and the fabric of reality. In some cases, spending your life learning a particular hex formula could be worth it."

Time and space? The fabric of reality? So would that mean that you could connect places through space and control time?

I couldn't even begin to fathom it.

"That's all sorts of confusing," I muttered.

Magic was definitely more convenient because of its wide range of uses, but that didn't mean you could just write sorcery off, no matter how nonsensical it may seem on the surface.

"Nobody uses sorcery anymore, so I never would have imagined we'd find a book like this here," said Amako, putting the book on a random shelf.

"Really?" I asked. "Nobody?"

"In the past, sorcery was seen as similar to Mana Boosting, but not anymore. I mean, it makes so much more sense to perfect the magic you have than to spend decades trying to decipher something you may never actually understand, right?"

"Yeah, that makes a lot of sense."

For humans, sorcery was a skill with too many drawbacks. Learning it was so difficult that humans probably just abandoned the idea. However, the enemy we were hunting this evening wasn't human.

"What's the lifespan of a necromancer?" I asked.

"It's multiple times that of a human," replied Amako.

"I thought so."

It was a monster, after all, so it wasn't all that surprising to hear it lived several times longer than a human.

"The worst thing is that we don't know what sorcery is written in that book, and we can't work it out," I said.

"Yep. If we knew what sorcery it was, we might be able to work out a countermeasure, but for now . . . we'll just have to approach the necromancer knowing that sorcery is one of its options."

I nodded. We might not know exactly what sorcery the necromancer had at its disposal, but we knew for sure that it was not to be underestimated. As far as I could tell, it looked like my fight against Halpha at Luqvist would make a good reference.

The plan was simple: hit the necromancer where it was weak before it had a chance to put any of its sorcery to use.

"Good plan, Usato," I muttered to myself.

"Well, let's move on to the other rooms," said Amako.

"Good call."

There didn't seem to be any more useful information regarding the necromancer in this room anyway.

But what is this jitter I feel in my chest?

"Let's hurry," I said.

"Okay."

What influence would this strange sorcery have on us?

Thinking about it filled me with a strange nervousness, but all the same, Amako and I put the study behind us and kept on searching for the necromancer.

* * *

Sir Usato and Miss Amako had just entered the manor. The villagers and I had drawn the zombies to us, and with me and my fire magic in the lead, we were taking them down. Fortunately, nobody had been hurt as we led the zombies away from the manor.

"Something doesn't feel right," I muttered.

I wasn't unhappy that the plan was going so smoothly, but it was extremely strange. The zombies were moving exactly the way we wanted them to. I couldn't put my finger on exactly why, and that made me anxious.

"It's like we're being tested," I said as I cut down an attacking zombie with my flaming sword.

I looked around at the villagers pushing the zombies back with their farming tools while others chopped off limbs to render the zombies immobile. Many of the zombies were no longer a threat, but they were still coming. I wiped the sweat from my brow as the village chief, wielding an old sword of his own, spoke.

"You truly *are* powerful, Aruku," he said.

"I couldn't handle all of these zombies on my own," I replied. "It's because of everyone's support that I can wield my sword freely."

And it really was thanks to them. As long as they had my back, I didn't have to worry about surprise attacks. I could focus my strength on the zombies in front of me. And as long as I could concentrate with such ease, even someone as clumsy as myself could keep the villagers protected.

"I wonder how Usato is doing," said the village chief.

"He'll be fine," I replied.

"You trust him."

"I do. He's my friend."

I knew that he was a warrior. I had seen him running through the battlefield in the battle against the Demon Lord's forces. But he wasn't just physically tough; Usato's mental fortitude meant that he would not yield to anyone. I didn't think for an instant that he would be caught off guard by a mere necromancer.

"You think very highly of him. Just who *is* that young man?"

Who, indeed?

"He's a healer," I said.

Usato had hidden the fact that he was a healer, but I would tell everyone for him. I would tell them all about him, and I would not leave out the fact that he was a healer. I knew that the chief and the villagers here with me would not look down on us because of such a fact.

"Wow, so he's a healer," muttered the village chief.

"Are you disappointed?" I asked.

"Not at all. Quite the opposite."

I tilted my head as I sent more zombies packing. The village chief's comment confused me.

"Before we set out, he told me that he was good at first aid magic and would heal anyone who was injured."

"Ah, I see."

"I was quite surprised. He was about to march off into danger, and yet he showed us all great kindness."

I couldn't help but laugh.

"That's Sir Usato for you."

That was just who he was.

"No ordinary young man would say such a thing so casually. No ordinary healer, for that matter. I feel certain that Usato has overcome considerable adversary for one so young."

"Indeed."

I thought back to when I had seen Sir Usato during the war. My duty was to defend the rescue team, and so I had seen both Lady Rose and Sir Usato leave the rescue team camp together.

Lady Rose was a woman of such caliber that in terms of strength and healing she was peerless in the Llinger Kingdom.

And yet, with Sir Usato by her side, I felt a light from him not unlike that of Rose herself—powerful and bright. In the two of them, I saw the very definition of master and disciple.

To enter a warzone—where attack magic and weapons assaulted you at every turn—took incredible grit. It was not something one could do without first having a steely resolve. And yet, the young Sir Usato never faltered as he followed Lady Rose onto the battlefield. When I saw him there, running out into battle, I trembled at the sheer emotion of it all.

In that moment, I knew without a sliver of uncertainty what Usato was.

"He is a hero," I said. "For us and for all of the Llinger Kingdom."

I believed that with every fiber of my being.

People were now alive thanks to his efforts. People who could cry and laugh and smile. It was an easy thing to slaughter another in battle, but it was not so easy to save a life. For that, Sir Usato was a hero, just as all the members of the rescue team were.

"I feel it is an honor that I get to travel alongside Sir Usato on his journey," I said.

I realized then that perhaps I'd been talking too much. It was perhaps a good time for us to go and support Usato's efforts. If he and Amako hadn't found the necromancer yet, we might still be able to help them. I told the village chief behind me to get ready to move on the manor.

"Once we clear the zombies here, let's enter the manor," I said. "There may still be more lurking inside."

But I was met with silence.

"Chief?" I asked.

Just as I turned to see what was going on, the chief's sword handle came down upon my wrist, and I dropped my sword.

"What the?!"

I couldn't believe what had just happened. I instinctively tried to create some distance, but before I could, the villagers had my arms and legs pinned.

"Grr! What is this?!" I shouted at the village chief. "Are you traitors?! No, wait, you're . . .?!"

But his eyes were completely empty, and he was suddenly much, much stronger than a man of his years. All of the villagers were the same. I couldn't even move.

"You're all being controlled!"

It was not the villagers who had walked me into a trap. It was whoever was *controlling* them.

But that means that from the moment we entered the village . . .

"No, Sir Usato!"

I have to warn them! He and Miss Amako are probably still in the manor!

I tried to shout but the villagers forced me to my knees.

"Just as I thought," said someone from behind me. "How fascinating."

I could not turn to face the speaker, but its voice sent a shiver down my spine as it approached. I suddenly realized that the surrounding zombies had frozen and were simply staring at someone behind me, as if waiting for commands.

"You can control the living?!" I shouted.

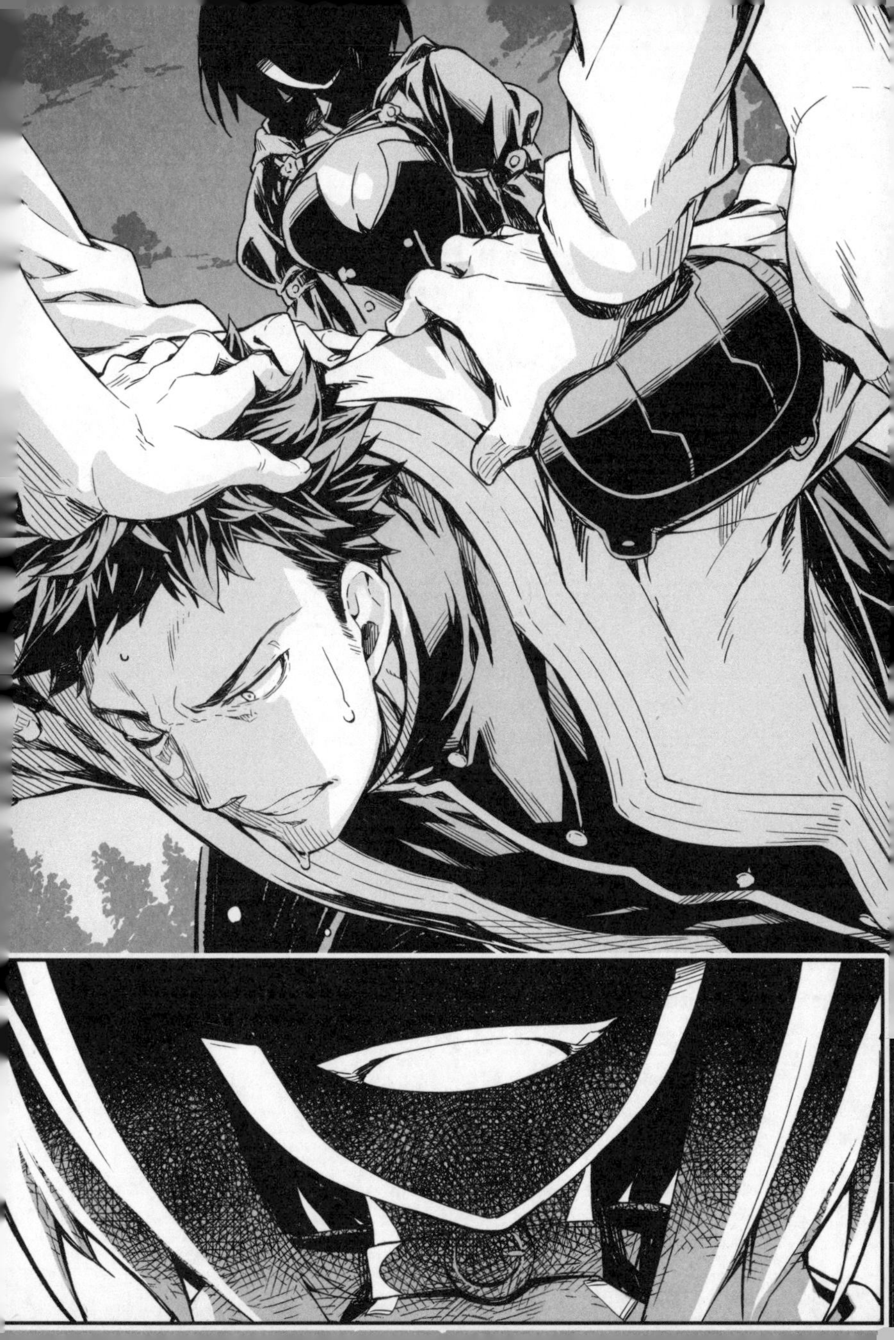

I knew of only one monster that could do such a thing. But we were supposed to be facing a necromancer. The zombies it now controlled were proof of that.

No! Is that even possible?!

"So that's . . . why!" I spat.

"How exciting! A hero, you say? I am *so* intrigued!"

One of the villagers then held my head tight to expose the flesh on my neck.

"You seem like the most troublesome of the lot," said the voice, giggling.

"Don't you dare . . . touch them!"

But the girl behind me continued to giggle.

"Relax," she said. "I'm going to catch them just like I did you."

She drew nearer and sunk her fangs into my neck. In an instant, the power drained from my body, and my consciousness faded. I moaned as I realized I was being hypnotized and put under control. And if this girl was what I thought she was, then it no longer mattered what I wanted—I would do her bidding.

I could struggle no longer.

"Sir Usato . . . Miss Amako . . ." I muttered. "I'm . . . sorry. If I'd only realized . . . sooner . . ."

The villagers released me, and I slumped to the ground. As my consciousness began to fade away, I saw a girl before me, her eyes blood red. She had a spine-chilling grin on her face.

The Wrong Way To Use Healing Magic 4

CHAPTER 5

Shock! Trust Betrayed!

Upon leaving the study, we went through all the manor's remaining rooms with a fine-tooth comb . . . which is to say, Amako stood in front of each room's closed door, and she used her magic to tell me whether or not we needed to bother with going inside. It was a simple, direct method and easily our best course of action. We didn't have time to search every room while Aruku and the villagers were holding off the zombies outside.

Unfortunately, we couldn't find the necromancer anywhere.

"Amako, what about here?" I asked.

Amako stood in front of the big set of double doors and used her magic, just as she'd done many times now. After a few seconds of staring at the door, she shook her head.

"The room is too big. I can't see anything from outside like this."

"Well then, let's check it out ourselves," I said.

It had to be the biggest room in the entire manor. It was located in the middle of the third floor, and it really jumped out at you—you couldn't miss it. I didn't expect that we'd find the necromancer here.

I let out a little sigh and pushed the doors open.

"Wow, it really *is* big," I said.

The doors opened into a giant hall. There was an expensive carpet on the floor and a chandelier that looked completely out of place in all the darkness, but other than that, the room was empty.

"Well, there's nowhere for the necromancer to hide in here, so . . . uh, Amako?"

Amako was frozen in place, staring at the room.

"Did you see something with your magic?" I asked.

Amako said nothing.

"Are you okay, Amako?" I asked.

When she still didn't reply, I gave her shoulders a light shake and she snapped back to reality with a quiver.

"Wh-what? What's going on?" she asked.

"That's what *I* want to know. Did you just see something with your magic?"

Amako hesitated for a moment, then shook her head.

"It's nothing. I was just spacing out," she replied.

"If you're not feeling well, let me know, okay? I'll probably freak out if you suddenly collapse or something."

"Got it."

She smiled as we left the hall.

Is she really okay? That didn't look like a girl who was just spacing out. It looked like something really bothered her. I don't like it.

"Well, we've searched pretty much everywhere," I said as we made our way down from the third floor.

"Usato, that hall we were in before . . ." said Amako.

She seemed suddenly hesitant, like she was reluctant to speak.

"Yeah?"

"Uh, actually, it's nothing."

What did she sense back there? It just looked like a big room to me, but perhaps I missed something?

I kept an eye on Amako and thought about our current circumstances. It was possible that the necromancer had already run away. I didn't know exactly how it had noticed us, but based on the study we visited—which was lit up and filled with stuff—we knew that *something* had been in the manor. Perhaps it had noticed us at some point and made a break for it.

That was the most natural explanation, but it felt a little too early to jump to any conclusions, so we kept searching.

"This is all that's left," I muttered.

It was a door built into the floorboards, on the first floor.

"Maybe it was for food storage?" I said. "In any case, let's take a look."

I opened the door quietly. Dust and mold drifted up from the basement along with a strange, unpleasant stench. It was like a mix of beasts, rotten meat, and moldy air—really awful stuff.

"What is that?" I asked, coughing. "Maybe there are some dead animals or something down there. Amako, are you okay?"

"I'm okay, but it stinks."

Amako covered her nose with her cloak and looked past the open door. It was pitch black down there. With what little light we had, it was impossible to see just how big the basement area was.

Well, let's take a peek for starters.

I opened the door fully, then got down on my hands and knees to peek inside. It was so dark that even when I squinted my eyes for a better look, I saw almost nothing.

"Hm? There's something big down there . . ."

I couldn't make it out clearly, but the silhouette I saw was definitely something.

Probably best to get Amako to check this out, seeing as she can see in the dark.

"Amako, could you take a look? Not with your magic, just normally."

"Okay."

Amako nodded and peered down through the door. I couldn't make out anything, but perhaps she'd see what was down there with her beastkin eyes. I felt a presence down there. Maybe there were ancient antiques in the basement.

Then Amako gasped.

"Amako?" I asked.

But when I looked at her, she was shaking so badly that her hands slipped.

"Whoa!" I cried, grabbing her cloak to make sure she didn't fall straight down into the basement. "What's wrong? This isn't like you . . . huh?!"

Amako suddenly wrapped herself around one of my arms.

Is this like a 'hug Usato day' or something?

The thought was completely irrelevant. I was going to make a remark about Amako, but then I thought better of it—she was trembling like crazy.

"Amako, what's . . . wait. What did you see down there?"

Whatever it was, it had shocked her so badly that she now had her face buried in my chest. That thing in the basement had inspired a serious level of fear in her.

"Should I go check it out?" I asked.

There was a chance that what was down there might harm the villagers. Maybe if I brought down one of the magical lamps from the study, I could see. But as I tried to stand up, I felt the silent Amako grip my arm even tighter. When she looked up at me, I could see in her eyes that she was terrified.

"Usato . . ." she muttered. "Don't go . . ."

"Whatever it is, we have to check it out," I said.

"But I saw it. It looked at me."

Who did? Or should I say . . . what?

"It's not a living creature," Amako said. "It's something different. Something way scarier. I've seen a lot of things on my travels, but never anything like that. So please . . . don't go in there."

"Okay."

Amako was still clinging to me desperately, so I reluctantly agreed to do as she said. I still thought it was best we check it out, and the sooner the better, but I knew I couldn't leave Amako like this either. I slowly closed the basement door and turned to face Amako.

"It's okay," I said. "We'll go look elsewhere."

I'd really screwed up. Even though I didn't know what was down there, I'd shown Amako something that shook her to her core. And while she often acted older than she was, at the end of the day, she was still just a fourteen-year-old girl.

"I've still got a lot to learn," I muttered, standing up.

I was disappointed in myself for not being more aware of such things and more prepared. Fortunately, Amako looked a little calmer. She let go of my arm apologetically.

"I'm sorry," she said, "for being so insistent about it . . ."

"Don't worry. I'm not so narrow minded that I'll get angry at you about something like that."

"But you always get angry about little things."

That's because you're always shooting off your mouth.

I could see the pout on her face, but I turned my attention back to the necromancer hunt.

"We've searched pretty much every room," I said. "Once we finish up, let's regroup with Aruku."

But where was the necromancer? Did a necromancer even

exist here in the first place? All we knew for sure was that someone or something definitely lived here. I also didn't think that the villagers had been lying to us.

"So much we still don't know," I muttered, pressing my closed eyes with my fingers.

"Huh?" said Amako, looking puzzled as she put a hand to one of her ears.

"What is it?"

"I can't hear Aruku and the others outside anymore."

"What?"

I looked over at the door leading outside and strained to listen.

Aruku and the villagers had been drawing the zombies away, but all of a sudden . . . they'd gone completely silent. The distant sounds of battle had disappeared.

"Is it possible that they've put a stop to all the zombies?" asked Amako.

"I don't know. It seemed like there were too many for them to dispatch *that* quickly."

I didn't like thinking about it, but maybe Aruku and the villagers had instead fallen to the zombies. I had a bad feeling growing inside of me. I decided it was time for a change of plan.

"Let's go check on Aruku and the others!" I said.

"Okay!"

We ran over to the door. Finding the necromancer was important, but not as important as our friends and allies! The moment I put a hand to the doorknob, however, a bunch of tree branch-like arms pushed through the gap, and zombies began forcing their way inside. Amako shrieked.

"An ambush?!" I shouted.

I launched a straight kick at the zombie in the lead as it tried to push through the door. It barreled into the zombies behind it and rolled along the floor.

"Amako! Don't move!"

"Huh? Wha? Huh?!"

I took the frozen Amako in my arms and backed away. Zombie voices filled the air all around us.

Where were they all hiding?

"This is going to get a little bumpy!" I said.

"What?!"

We had to get out of here, immediately. With Amako under one of my arms, I dodged the incoming zombies and dashed up the stairs. Fortunately, there weren't any zombies waiting for us on the higher floors. I kicked open the door into the third-floor hall. It was still as deserted as it was when we'd last seen it, and there wasn't a zombie in sight.

"They're going to corner us, Usato!" cried Amako.

Here on the third floor, there was nowhere else to run. If we tried to go back the way we came, we'd be surrounded by zombies in no time. I sighed.

"What do we do?" asked Amako. "Should I use my magic to find a weak point in the zombie forces for us to break through?"

"No need for that," I replied. "I know a quicker escape."

Based on where all the zombies had come from, I felt like they were all intentionally herding us up towards the third floor, where there was no escape. But whoever was controlling them had made a mistake.

Do you have any idea who my teacher was? She literally threw me off a cliff pretty much the moment I started understanding how my magic worked. You think a measly three floors is going to spook **me***?*

"Don't you dare think that three floors are going to be enough to stop me," I muttered.

"Wait, Usato, wait," said Amako, her voice trembling.

She watched as I opened the windows onto the balcony. Still in my arms, she looked up at me, her face pale as a sheet as she shook her head.

"So you are a girl after all," I said with a chuckle.

"This has nothing to do with being a girl!" cried Amako.

Oh look at you, so adorable with your fear of heights. But there's no other way to escape, so strap yourself in.

To try and put Amako at ease, I grinned at her.

"You can't be serious, Usato," said Amako, her expression a portrait of despair.

I knew I wasn't going to be able to make a solid landing

with Amako tucked under my arm, so I hoisted her around and held her in both arms. Then I stepped back from the window to give us a bit of a run-up.

"Don't worry," I said. "I won't let you go. I promise."

"It doesn't matter what you say!"

"Here we go! Keep your mouth shut so you don't bite your own tongue!"

"Are you even listening to me?!"

I took off running and jumped from the third-floor balcony. Amako screamed as we flew through the air. There were no zombies below us. We landed at a point some fifteen meters from the manor proper. I felt a slight numbness work its way through my body—carrying another person was tougher on my legs than I expected.

Still, I breathed a sigh of relief.

"Escape attempt successful," I said.

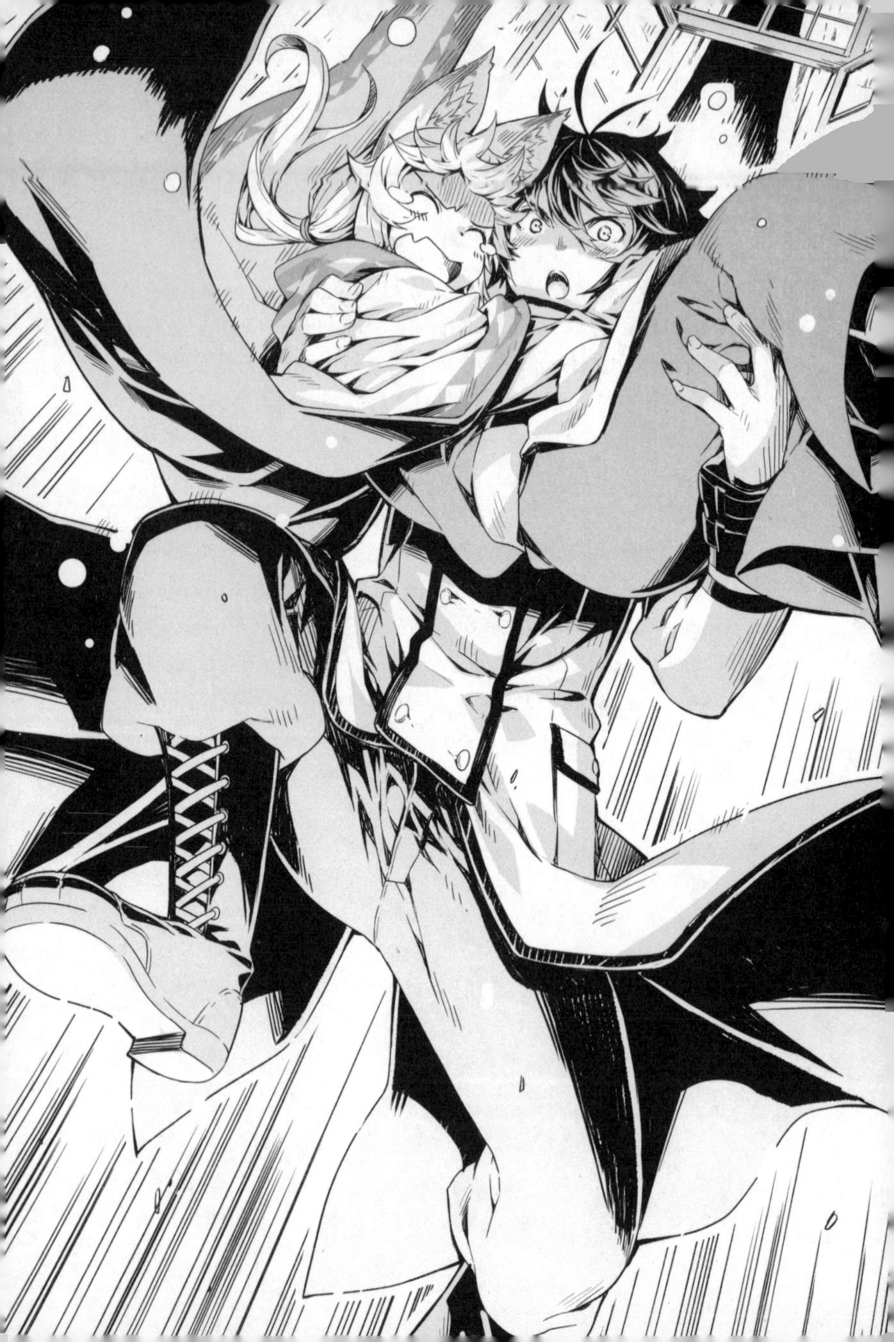

I quickly shot some healing through Amako's body. There were no zombies around the manor anymore.

"I guess all of the zombies are inside," I said. "Now is a good opportunity for us to find the others. Can you walk?"

"Th-th-th-that was so scary . . ."

"Oh, you poor thing," I said.

The zombies terrified her, the poor girl.

Amako was still stammering as I put her down on the ground and looked out at the path to the village.

"Where did everyone go?"

There was no way that Aruku would have abandoned us, so I had to assume that he ran into some kind of trouble. I looked around the area carefully, then found someone slumped over near the edges of the forest.

"Aruku?!" I shouted.

There was a little blood running from his neck. He was lying on the ground and so fast asleep that he looked dead. I dashed over to him and immediately cast healing magic.

"Are you okay?!"

But even after I'd healed him back to health, Aruku still didn't wake up. On top of that, the more we tried talking to him, the more he moaned something we couldn't understand. I looked at the two little scars on his neck. It was like something had bit him.

"Something happened to him . . ." I said. "And where did all the villagers go?"

I couldn't see any of them anywhere.

"Perhaps they all ran away," said Amako, a pained look on her face. "Perhaps they left Aruku all by himself."

It was possible. The more likely possibility was that Aruku had helped them all get away, then fought as best he could on his own. Then, while he had his hands full with zombies, a stronger enemy emerged out of nowhere.

But that would mean . . .

My thoughts were interrupted by a shuffling in the bushes.

"Is it zombies?!"

I put up my fists, ready for a fight. But instead of zombies, villagers emerged from the forest. Amako immediately hid behind me and put her hood back on.

"It's the village chief!" I said. "Are you all okay?"

"Yes, but . . . more importantly, how's Aruku?"

"I've healed his wounds, but I'm not sure. What happened?"

The village chief frowned as he explained to us that another monster had attacked them while they were fighting the zombies. It was extremely strong, and the villagers' weapons had been completely ineffective. Aruku had put the safety of the villagers first. He told them to flee while he attempted to fight the monster on his own.

"I'm so sorry!" said the village chief. "We did not have the strength to protect Aruku!"

But something about the story didn't sit right with me.

Yeah, it was certainly true that Aruku would put the villagers first. But was that really what happened? Aruku was a gatekeeper at Llinger Kingdom. He was proud of his job, and if push came to shove and he had to really fight, he would have used his fire magic to its fullest potential.

And yet, there were no signs of battle anywhere near him. The scene didn't make any sense. When he'd fought the zombies with his flaming sword, he'd left charred marks along the ground. I'd seen them myself.

The other thing that bothered me was that the bite marks were on his clavicle. For a monster to bite him there, it would have had to attack him from behind. I couldn't ever imagine Aruku giving up his back so easily.

"Leave the rest of this to us and head back to the village," I said. "I'll carry Aruku."

"U-Usato . . ." started the village chief.

"We still haven't found the necromancer. The monster that attacked Aruku may still be lurking around here somewhere too. It was clearly powerful enough to catch him off guard. That means it could well prove difficult for me to fight—if I have to protect you all at the same time."

The village chief and his accompanying villagers were all confused by what I said. I didn't know if it was because they were worried about being attacked, or because they hadn't expected me to say what I did. In any case, my job now was to hide Aruku and Amako in the bushes where nobody would find them and crush all the zombies' limbs so they couldn't get revenge by attacking the village.

I didn't much like the work ahead of me, but I knew I had to do what I had to do.

"Go," I said. "Hurry back to the village and tell your families it will be alright."

I was met by silence.

"Hm?"

Just then, I froze. It was as if my body, arms, and legs had been bound by something.

"What the?!" I exclaimed.

I can't move?

To be more precise, my body was frozen from the neck down. When I looked down at it, I saw black patterns emitting a purple light that stretched across my body and each of my limbs. The patterns flowed across my body, keeping me completely locked down.

What is this?!

Amako quickly noticed something was off and approached me.

"Usato? What's wrong?!" asked Amako.

But then I saw a group of nearby villagers moving in to attack her.

"Amako!" I shouted.

Amako heard the warning in my voice and quickly jumped away from me, out of reach of the villagers.

What are they doing?! I can't even move my body to help her!

"Usato! The villagers! They're not conscious of what they're doing!"

"What? You mean they're being controlled?!"

But necromancers can only control the dead! The villagers are all living, breathing humans!

Then I heard someone giggling. It wasn't the village chief, nor was it any of the villagers. It came from the third-floor balcony that Amako and I had just jumped from. A figure was sitting there as if it were the most natural thing in the world, looking down at me and giggling derisively.

As the moon peeked out from behind the clouds, it bathed the entire manor in moonlight, and revealed the figure on the balcony.

"Nea . . . ?" I uttered.

"Hiya Usato!"

It was Nea smiling down at us. But this was not the girl I had talked to earlier. The Nea on the balcony had jet black hair. Her eyes glimmered with a suspicious red in the darkness. She was in a black dress and her aura was completely different from earlier.

I couldn't hide my confusion.

"Why . . . are you . . . ?" I stammered.

"But surely *that's* obvious," replied Nea, daring me with her eyes.

Until everything went south, we'd been searching the manor for the necromancer. Given that Nea was acting like the place was home, the answer was like a slap in the face. The necromancer wasn't a man at all.

"So, *you* did this to Aruku?" I asked.

Nea giggled.

"You're much calmer about this than I expected. I thought you'd be so much more panicked."

To be honest, I wanted to be more panicked, but my body was bound by something, and I still didn't know what.

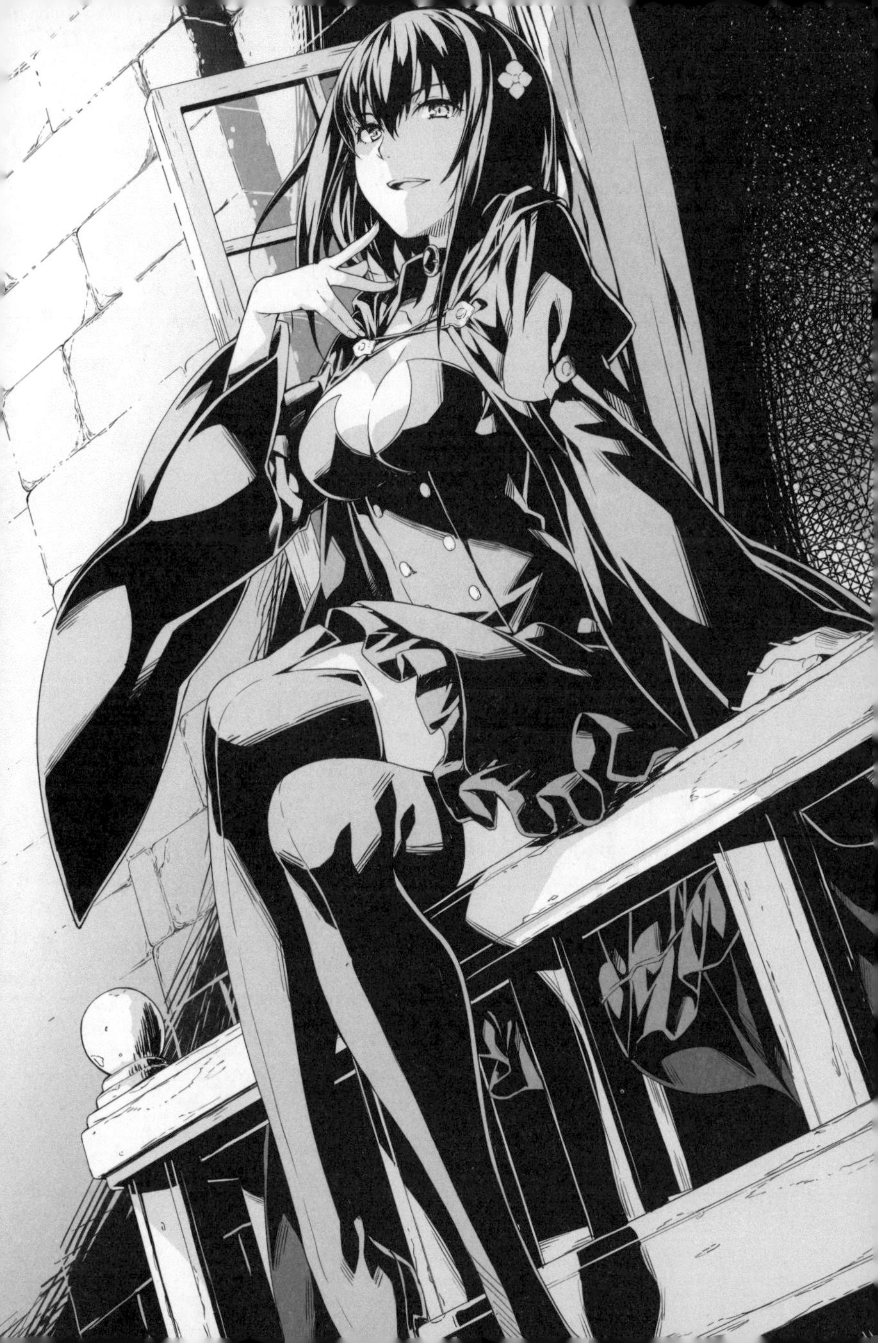

Unfortunately, this was not a good time for me to be completely frozen. If the villagers really were under Nea's control, then I had no way of defending myself from them. I shouted to Amako, who was a little ways behind me.

"Amako! Run!"

"Wh-what are you saying?! If I run then you'll—"

"Forget about me!"

"No! Without you, I . . ."

It was nice that she was worried, but there was no way Amako was going to just pick me up and get the both of us to safety.

"You have to get away from here! Aruku and I are helpless! How else are we going to get out of this?!"

"Hngh!" grunted Amako. "Fine! Okay!"

She finally seemed to get it. She nodded hesitantly and ran toward the village. The villagers, however, remained frozen. I glanced at them, then back up to Nea, who looked like she was having a ball.

"You're not going after her?" I asked.

"Hm. I'll get her later. Beastkin are interesting and all, but all she's got going for her is heightened senses."

That's right! Nea doesn't know what Amako's magic is. Glad we kept that under wraps.

If we hadn't, Nea might well have gone for Amako first.

"So what did you do to me?" I asked.

"I merely locked your ability to move. Keeping you under control with the zombies and the villagers was never going to be easy, even if we caught you by surprise."

So saying, Nea looked supremely pleased with herself as she showed me the palm of her hand. An ominously glowing pattern floated from her hand, just like the one that had me all wrapped up.

"What is that?"

"It's called the binding hex. Making it is incredibly, like *incredibly*, hard, and it takes forever. But in return, it wraps the target up extremely tight."

So that's why I'm frozen like this?

"I meant it when I said it was hard, by the way," continued Nea. "I had to put pretty much all of my magical power into it. *And* it took six hours! That's the effort I put into this. Not that you'd ever really understand what I mean."

Nea made the seal on her palm disappear, then floated gently down from the balcony. Black, bat-like wings appeared from her back, carrying her softly down to the ground. That was when I knew for certain that Nea wasn't human.

She'd cast her hex on me before we came here, when she'd hugged me. I'd thought it was strange for her to hug me like that out of the blue, and now I knew that it was all for the sake of this hex. I was at a loss for words.

"So this is sorcery, huh?" I said. "It's just as strong as I've heard."

But that power came at a significant cost—both in terms of time and energy. It wasn't easy to use, either—not when you considered the sheer effort Nea had put into it. But while I was looking down at my body and thinking about sorcery, Nea tilted her head, suddenly confused.

"How do you know that it's sorcery?" she asked.

Oh.

"Someone left a book of sorcery lying around in the manor study, and the lights were on in there. We couldn't miss it."

"Are you serious? I forgot to turn the lights off?"

"Huh?"

"Forget about it. So I don't need to explain it, I suppose. That's right—I'm a monster capable of sorcery."

I guess even as a monster she's a bit of an airhead. And even though she's my enemy now, it's still kind of adorable.

"So you're a monster then? Really?" I asked.

I still couldn't hide my surprise at discovering that an ordinary girl we'd met at Ieva Village was in fact a monster. Even as she walked toward me, she still looked human. Nea seemed to enjoy my puzzled gaze—I could see it in her smile.

"There *are* monsters that look just like humans, you know. They're rare, but still."

"So that means . . . *you're* the necromancer?"

"You're half-right. An ordinary necromancer wouldn't be able to control the living."

The village chief and the villagers were all still alive, and yet under her control. It was possible that they were all already dead, but when I'd talked to the village chief and the villagers earlier, they'd definitely been alive.

But there was no monster in the book Rose gave me that could control living people.

"I'm half necromancer and half another monster."

"Is that even possible?"

"Procreation isn't always limited to within a set species. I'm a very unique case—my mother was a necromancer, who can control the dead, and my father was something different. His power let him control the living. I get the best of both worlds."

A monster that controls the living?

Suddenly, a monster came to mind—one that could control the living, had wings like a bat, and sucked blood from people's necks. It was, admittedly, a bit on the dramatic side, however.

"Listen in awe, as I reveal that I am the progeny of a necromancer and a—"

"Wait, you're not going to say vampire, are you?"

Nea froze, her smile still plastered to her face. I felt suddenly apologetic.

"I'm sorry," I said.

But a hybrid of a necromancer and a vampire? That really is the best of both worlds. Well, given my current predicament, it's actually the worst . . .

The fictional vampires of my home world and the vampires of this world seemed to share some similarities—blood sucking, incredible strength, and the ability to shape shift.

Nea giggled.

"You really are a curious one, aren't you? You're completely frozen, completely unable to move, and yet you clearly don't fear me in the slightest. Even given your circumstances, you still have the gall to talk back to me."

"Let's not get ahead of ourselves, I'm not anything special. Just another ordinary healer, right here."

As for the lack of fear, well, I'd developed a resistance thanks to the time I'd spent living with something that was truly terrifying.

Nea seemed to think my reply was funny. She covered her mouth as she burst into laughter.

"Not anything special? Oh, I doubt that. You need more than just higher-than-average physical abilities to take out my underlings. You also completely resisted my charm. I couldn't believe it.

"Charm?"

"Bewitching. It's a vampiric ability. Most people fall head over heels and melt for me. Where the heck did you learn such mental fortitude? Nobody 'ordinary' can just shake it off."

So all those times I felt a spark between us, it was just Nea's bewitching?

"You monster! I can't believe you'd do that!"

"Um . . . why does *that* bother you more than me tricking you about all the other stuff?"

This is what happens when you toy with a guy's innocence! His emotions!

But now I realized that the whole thing started with the very first zombie attack. We fell for it hook, line, and sinker and kept on doing everything expected of us.

"So what are you going to do with me now?" I asked.

"I'm going to make you my conversation partner."

"Are you for real?"

"What else would I do?"

Why would *anyone* go that far for that reason? They wouldn't. There had to be another reason.

No way . . .

"You're going to make me a source of sustenance," I uttered. "You're going to use my healing powers to your advantage so that you have an endless blood tank. I should have known that a vampire would come up with something so grotesque!"

Nea looked plainly offended. It seemed clear that the endless blood tank was *not* her intention.

"So what, then?" I asked. "You did all of this just for someone to talk to?"

"That's what I said, didn't I? Now, while blood *is* delicious to vampires like me, we're not exactly bloodthirsty, either. Blood is like wine for us. It's all about moderation, right?"

Maybe I'm not the right guy to look for affirmation on this point? I've never touched wine in my life. That's a very foreign concept to me.

"So blood *isn't* the main source of sustenance for vampires?"

"I eat and drink the same as any ordinary human," said Nea. "And blood is all the same, you know. It's just a matter of whether it's fresh or not. The idea of making something so bland your sole source of nourishment? That's just crazy."

My whole understanding of vampires was crumbling before my eyes.

"In any case, that might be because I'm only half vampire."

"Being a hybrid would change you *that* much?" I asked.

"Yes. Look at it this way—I have none of the vampire's and the necromancer's weaknesses. I was born with only their strengths."

"The best of both worlds, as you say."

I didn't know about necromancers, but I guess all the well-known vampire remedies were out—sunlight, running water, garlic, that kind of thing.

I'd been caught by a foe who was way more of a handful than I had expected.

How am I going to get out of this?

"You look pretty relaxed for someone bound and powerless," remarked Nea.

She was close enough to touch me now. She looked up at me as she gently put a hand to my cheek.

"You didn't have to do all of this if you just wanted to talk," I said. "You could have just asked."

"But then you would have left soon, no?"

I said nothing.

"Humans as unique as you are so very rare. You can defeat a zombie with your bare hands, you've been given an important duty to carry out, and your friend calls you a hero. I had to make sure you wouldn't get away."

I was exactly what she was looking for. With her hand still on my cheek, she brought my gaze in line with her own.

"I desire knowledge," she said. "Not the stuff written on paper or in books, but the lives that people lead—I want to know the memories they have of their travels. But I don't want just anyone. I want to know *you*. I want to know the life you've lived, and the trials you overcame, and how you came to wield such monstrous strength."

"But I might not open up to you about it."

"Oh, you will. You will because I'll simply order you to do so."

With a smile, Nea flashed her fangs. She wanted to bite my neck, just like she had Aruku's. And if I was bitten, would that make me just like the puppet villagers standing around us?

"Wait," I said. "How long have you been doing this for?"

"Hm, for about two hundred years? That's about how long I've been playing this villager act too."

That explained all the armor inside of the manor, then. All this time, Nea had done this over and over—making people her slaves and wiping their memories so they didn't realize what had happened. Nea was behind all of the rumors that Aruku had shared with me.

"What about Tetra, then?" I asked.

"Tetra? Oh, I'm like a mother to her."

If she was like a mother to Tetra, did that mean she was capable of mercy and compassion? Perhaps there was a way for me to talk to her and turn her around.

"Oh, don't get the wrong idea," said Nea, before I could start.

"About what?"

"You're hoping that if a girl like me will play mother to a human, then perhaps I'm a monster with a kinder, gentler side to me, yeah?"

I did not answer. She'd hit the nail on the head.

"I'm not like that at all. Tetra and everyone else at the village, they're all just a cover for me—just a way for me to blend in as a young villager."

That meant she was using the villagers for her own purposes—so she could kidnap the people who visited.

"What are the villagers to you?" I asked.

"They're my puppets," replied Nea. "They feel what I want them to feel. Their memories are what I want them to be. When I told you I didn't have parents, I was lying. When I said that Tetra was like a mother to me, that was a lie too. I've imprinted her with memories that make her think of me as her own daughter. It's hilarious."

I couldn't believe that she could say all of that so casually. It was insane. She was merciless—she was bending people's lives to her will. She didn't think anything of humans—they were nothing more than toys to her.

"Fine. I'll be your conversation partner," I said.

"Oh? If I don't have to keep tight control over you, this will all be so much easier."

I just didn't want to be her partner *now*.

"Can I come back once I've finished my journey?"

"Hm?"

Nea tilted her head.

"We're traveling because we have a very important job to do. Like I told you yesterday, the fate of the world is at stake. So, can you wait until we're done? You can cast whatever sorcery hex you like to ensure that I come back."

Of course, I'd be coming for a fight. I'd bring the true Demon Lord, Rose, and all of the rescue team, and we'd turn Nea's manor into dust.

I didn't know how Nea was going to take my offer, but with

my cheeks still in her hands, she squealed and blushed.

"That's the first time anyone's ever said anything like that to me!" she exclaimed.

"It's not a profession of love! Don't get the wrong idea!"

That was beyond ridiculous. I was bound by her powers, after all!

Nea chuckled at my response.

"But no," she said. "I can't wait that long. I want to get inside that head of yours as soon as possible."

"The world is on the verge of crisis," I said.

"Why should a monster like me care about the Demon Lord?"

"You won't reconsider?"

"I won't!" replied Nea brightly.

"Wench, you are going to regret that decision," I murmured.

Whoops, I let my thoughts slip for a second there.

"Hm?"

"Uh, nothing?"

Phew, she didn't catch my comment.

Nea watched me closely. Talking wasn't getting us anywhere—Nea had *no* intention of letting me go.

"If you speak to me of your own volition, I might just release you earlier, you know."

"If I do as I'm told, like a good prisoner, then . . . how long are we talking?"

"Hm. When I lose interest? So probably not *that* long? I mean, people will start to notice you are missing if you're gone too long."

So in a sense, there was a kind of salvation in Nea's words. She would eventually let me go. Unfortunately, the part about her losing interest was straight-up awful for me. I mean, I was summoned from another world. There was no way of getting around that if I agreed to talk to Nea. Being that the unknown was like a rare treasure for Nea, I could be stuck as her prisoner my whole life just talking about the world I came from.

I have to avoid that at all costs!

"Is there no other way?" I asked.

"Why would you bother? Play nice and I'll let you go in no time. Isn't that what you want?"

I said nothing.

"I'm not hearing an answer."

Nea took a hold of my collar and pulled me closer. Because of the difference in our heights, she was still looking up at me, but our faces were almost touching as we stared into each others' eyes. She wasn't trying to bewitch me, but I could feel her gaze searching for something inside of me, and I could not look away.

"Once I've heard all about what you so clearly want to hide," she said with a giggle, "then I'll give you back your consciousness, and we can enjoy a cup of tea."

We stayed there staring at each other for what felt like a surprisingly long time, but it was perhaps just a few seconds. I didn't know. But when she was done, Nea gave a charming smile. It spread across her face as she moved around behind me. It was exactly what happened in the stories when the vampire was just about to sink its teeth into its prey.

"No, you don't!" I spat.

I strained with my right hand and heard a creaking sound as pain shot through me like an electric shock. I grunted and ignored it. I healed my pain and continued to struggle. A shot of pain followed by healing, over and over, and little by little, I felt the binds on my right arm grow weak—they were fracturing and starting to break.

"There we go!"

I wasn't completely mobile yet, but I had enough range of movement that I thrust my hand up and stopped Nea from biting my neck. Her fangs instead sunk into the back of my hand. Blood flowed from the wound, but I didn't notice any change in my body.

It looks like she has to get the neck if she wants to control somebody.

"Fwhat?! Fow?!" fumbled Nea, her fangs still stuck in my hand.

"I'm not so generous that I'll just let you at my neck!"

Nea leaped backward and created a little space between us. I wasn't sure if I'd be able to force my way out of these sorcery binds, but I figured it was worth a shot, and sure enough, I freed both my legs just like I did my right arm.

"Looks like all that hard work I put into training really *is* paying off," I uttered.

"Did you just *force* your way out . . . ? Are you serious?! Are you some kind of monster?!"

How rude!

"I'm a human!"

Blood dripped from Nea's mouth as she stood there dumbfounded, watching me run to Aruku. The binding hex was still activated, but I could at least move my legs somewhat, which meant I had options. The first order of business was getting a hold of Aruku and making a break for it.

"I won't let you get away that easily! After him!" cried Nea.

Before I could get to Aruku, the villagers pounced on me. I couldn't move well enough in my current state to fight back or even evade their attacks, so I gritted my teeth, charged into them, and dragged them all behind me as I worked my way toward Aruku.

"This is stupid! Just how insanely strong are you?!" Nea shouted.

"Ha. You think that *this* is enough to slow me down?"

I'm on the rescue team. This much weight is just another day at the office!

"That said, any more might be a little too much . . ." I muttered.

Just as I reached him, Aruku began to rise to his feet.

"Aruku!" I said. "You're awake! Will you give me a hand?"

Aruku said nothing.

"Oh. Wait, don't tell me—you're being controlled now?"

In response, Aruku tackled me to the ground.

"Not good, not good, not good!" I cried.

If Aruku had fallen into Nea's hands, we wouldn't be able to escape this place so easily. More to the point, *I* wouldn't even be able to escape the situation I was stuck in.

"Zombies!" commanded Nea. "Stop him in his tracks!"

I heard lumbering, shuffling footsteps exit from the manor doors. I looked over and saw countless zombies trudging toward us.

"Ugh," I muttered.

If those zombies got a hold of me, I'd be trapped.

It's all over.

But as soon as the word crossed my mind, a beastly roar filled the air. Nea was confused, but I knew exactly what it was.

"You finally made it!" I shouted.

With Aruku and I both unable to move, he was the only one with the strength to do anything. Amako knew it, and so when she'd disappeared, she'd run off to call for his help.

The footsteps drew nearer, and I knew what I had to say.

"Take them all down! Me included!"

A huge roar of a reply echoed around us as the blue grizzly,

Blurin, appeared. On his back, riding him, was Amako. Blurin must have understood what I'd shouted because he didn't stop for an instant and plowed into all of us—the villagers, Aruku, and me—and we went flying.

"Blurin, grab Usato!" cried Amako.

Blurin roared and ran underneath me, cushioning my fall. I landed face down and immediately looked up to express my thanks.

"Great job, partner! Amako, thank you!"

Blurin grunted as if to say, "You got it." I even thought I saw a smile on the grizzly's face.

"Usato, let's get out of here."

"But..."

I stopped myself from saying anything else. We couldn't save Aruku the way things were. Amako already knew this, and I could see her trying to keep her feelings under control by biting her lip.

"Nea!" I shouted, craning my neck around to look at her.

The vampiric necromancer was staring at us in a dumbfounded silence.

"Tomorrow night, I'm coming back for my friend," I declared, "so you can have him for now!"

Nea glared at me as Blurin carried us away. I looked over at the manor as it faded in the distance.

"We'll be back for you Aruku, I promise!"

The village had fallen under the control of a necromancer. But it was no longer really a village—that was merely a front. In truth, the place was now simply a way for Nea to indulge in her obsession with acquiring knowledge.

Now it was up to us to fight her—a fearsome enemy with the powers of both a necromancer and a vampire.

The Wrong Way To Use Healing Magic 4

CHAPTER 6

A Brief Moment of Respite!

We fled Nea's manor and hid in the nearby forest. With the villagers under Nea's control, the forest was the safest place for us. If we'd gone back to the village, we'd have only made ourselves clear targets.

Even though my healing punch was a nonlethal option, the villagers were innocent victims, and I didn't want to hurt them if I could avoid it. Also, when I'd been carried away on Blurin's back, I was still bound by Nea's hex.

I'd now seen firsthand how powerful sorcery was—I'd freed my right arm and both of my legs, but even then, I couldn't move the way I was used to. I knew there was no way I was going to be able to rescue Aruku in that state, so we opted to rest in the depths of the forest. I'd been exhausted from trying to negotiate with Nea, and more importantly, I'd pushed my body to its limits when I'd broken that hex.

"Morning already," I mumbled.

When I opened my eyes, the first thing I saw was a lazy, drooling Blurin. I felt unusually cozy. A quick look revealed that I'd been using Blurin as a pillow when I'd fallen asleep.

I instinctively reached out to push Blurin's head away with my left hand, then remembered the previous evening and instead gave the grizzly a gentle pat.

"I owe you one, buddy," I said.

The grizzly let out a pleasant moan. It made me happy.

Wait a sec, my left arm is . . . ?

"I can move it again," I exclaimed.

The magical seals that had bound me last night were gone. Was it possible that the binding hex had a time limit of some kind? I'd assumed that sorcery was something that persisted permanently, but I was glad and relieved to find that I was wrong. This, at least, meant I wouldn't have to spend time breaking free of them all.

I stood up and stretched to get a feel for my body. I found that I was in good shape. Nothing happened to me outside of the hex. In fact, I felt really well rested and, on top of that, like I'd gotten stronger somehow.

"No way," I said, laughing. "Are you telling me that Nea's binding hex helped me to . . . work out?"

I didn't like having my movements completely locked down, but I *did* have to admit that hexes were a surprisingly good workout.

"Anyway," I muttered to myself, "where's Amako?"

She'd come with us to the forest, but was it possible that she'd returned to the village by herself? No, she'd traveled a long way all on her own, and she was smarter than that. When it came to sensing the threat of danger, she was leagues above me. With that in mind, I leaned back against Blurin and waited for her to return.

Some ten minutes later Amako appeared from out of the nearby bushes. There were leaves in her hair, but she seemed otherwise fine.

"Can you move?" she asked.

"No need to worry about that," I said, swinging my arms around energetically. "As you can see, I'm doing great."

Amako looked relieved and opened her cloak, which she'd been using as a kind of makeshift bag. Inside of it was a collection of apple-like fruits, lots of them. Amako held one out to me.

"You're hungry, right?" she said.

"Wow! Thanks!" I replied.

I trusted that if Amako had found the fruit herself, they were fine to eat. I took the fruit in hand and cleaned it on my rescue team uniform before taking a bite. It filled my mouth with a unique fruity sweetness and acidity.

"This is good," I remarked.

Amako watched my reaction, then picked up a fruit of her own and took a bite.

"I figure if you can eat them without issue, then so can I."

"You really just used me as a poison check, didn't you?"

"Only because I trust you so completely."

*But this is what I get for trusting **you**? You do understand that even with my healing magic, I still feel pain, right? Right?*

I grumbled as I sat back down. Amako put a fruit in front of Blurin, then took a seat next to me.

"So, how are we going to save Aruku?" she asked.

"The zombies and the villagers are under Nea's control, but they're not anything for us to worry about," I said. "The real problem is Nea and her sorcery."

"Putting the sorcery aside," Amako said, "are Nea's innate monster abilities really all that much of an issue?"

Amako's question reminded me that she wasn't there when Nea revealed what she really was.

"She's a bit of a unique case . . ." I started.

I went on to explain to Amako exactly what Nea was. When I was done, Amako's face twisted with consternation.

"The child of a necromancer and a vampire? That's beyond even anything I could have imagined . . ." she uttered.

"Right?" I said, nodding.

I mean, talk about a surprise twist. Nea had literally been acting like a young village maiden for over two hundred years. Her teary-eyed words and her gratitude were all an act. All of it was part of her scheme. Even though I knew that, it still astonished me.

"She toyed with my feelings . . ." I muttered.

Amako said nothing in reply, but I could feel her icy gaze upon me. I pushed the thoughts away and put my focus back on Nea's abilities.

"The biggest issue now is that we don't know how hard Nea can fight," I said.

All we knew for certain was that her necromantic abilities let her raise and control the dead, and that her vampiric abilities let her suck people's blood and control them. Also, she could charm people by looking into their eyes, and she knew sorcery.

"That binding hex she trapped me with was tough, even for me," I admitted. "I think Blurin is probably *just* strong enough to deal with it, but you might find yourself completely unable to move if you're not careful."

"Yeah, I'll have to be on guard."

"However, there are certain conditions that have to be met for sorcery hexes to work. Nea didn't say it herself, but I'm pretty sure she has to touch the targets before she can cast a hex on them."

There was no other reason for her to have hugged me like she did before we left the village. And that meant that everything before the hug was carefully planned so that we'd let our guards down.

Fortunately, that made things very simple. The key was to not get touched. As long as I was in good condition, I could handle whatever villagers or zombies Nea tried to throw at me.

Still, there was one big problem—it was very possible that Nea knew more hexes than just the binding one she had cast. Seeing as she'd lived for two centuries, it wouldn't be surprising if she'd learned to master at least one or two more hexes.

"We don't know what other sorcery she can use," I said.

"But we'll never save Aruku if we let that stop us. Unfortunately, given Aruku's current state . . ."

"Under Nea's control, he might become our enemy."

"Yeah."

Aruku was now Nea's puppet. If the villagers were doing her bidding, then Aruku would be no different. I had to consider the worst-case scenario—that I might have to face off against Aruku, and he'd be going all out.

Wait a second. Aruku has been bitten, and now he's under Nea's control. But would she use him purely as a tool for battle? No. The first thing she'd do is go through his memories.

"Oh no . . ." I muttered.

"What?" asked Amako.

"Nea knows all about the both of us," I said.

She'd know that I was a human, summoned from another world, and she'd know that Amako was a beastkin with a very special magic. I had no idea what Nea would do with that information, but I knew one thing for sure—there was no way that Nea was going to give up and let us go now.

I heaved a great sigh. If Nea thought that I was just an unusually strong healer, then she wouldn't think I was all that valuable. Now that she knew I was from another world, however, she would probably do anything to catch me. This made things infinitely more troublesome.

"Well, nothing we can do about it now," I said, taking another fruit and biting into it.

All we could do was rest up and make sure we were as ready as possible.

"Oh, right," I said, suddenly remembering something.

It was the notebook in my rescue team coat. The one I'd taken from the manor. I reached into my pocket and pulled out the battered notebook. Amako's head tilted quizzically at the sight.

"What's that?" she asked.

"It's about the last generation's hero," I said, "I think."

I still hadn't taken a good look inside, so I couldn't be sure if it truly was about the hero. I didn't want to admit it, but it *was* possible that I'd never have another chance to read what was in this notebook, so I decided to look through it now.

I must make sure, first of all, that he does not find out about this record of his person. Should he discover my writings, he will most certainly dispose of them immediately. That is simply the extent to which he does not want himself known.

He refuses to let his weaknesses show.

Why?

The answer is simple—he has been made to believe only in strength and power. There is no meaning to anything else. If he is weak, none will need him, and he will be abandoned. Thrown away. As such, he shows not a single moment of weakness to anyone, and he continues to exude only power. He has never revealed his feelings, not even to me, his companion.

I regret that I did not try harder to know him better. To grow closer to him.

But my regret comes far too late, for his heart has already frozen completely.

His record of achievements is measured by the number of lives he has taken. He is praised for the vast number of corpses he has left in his wake, but for him this is a suffering beyond anything one can even imagine.

However, I have observed him all this time. I feel it is my duty to record what happened to him, so that the world will someday come to understand that he was vastly misunderstood.

The humans summoned one from another world to use them as a tool. The demi-humans were in need of a savior to revere. Neither is very different from the other, as far as I am concerned. Both of them placed everything on the shoulders of one individual, an individual who was entirely alone, with no friends, and none to understand him. Alone with no family, no home, and no place to go back to.

The humans and the demi-humans will both call him a hero, of that I am sure. But if someone is to read this text aside from myself, then I hope that at least you understand the truth. There is no mythical "hero". There is no human who does not fear death. The hero is a false idol, created by others.

And however powerful he becomes, he is still just a man.

A man with far too much placed on his shoulders.

You see, it does not matter if he parts the seas, or levels mountains, or kills dragons—he will always, at his heart, be human. And that is why I must leave this text for future generations—so that he does not go down as simply a hero, and so that I do not forget this regret in my heart.

What is written here is the record of a human, not a hero, and the sins we were to pay for in the far, far future.

I shut the notebook.

"That was *not* what I was expecting . . ." I muttered. "That was so, *so* dark . . ."

The notebook was so far from what I'd thought it would be that I couldn't even properly describe what I'd just read. When I flipped through the rest of the book, it was all about the hero's mental state and the tasks he had accomplished. I didn't know who wrote it, but clearly the writer was someone close to the hero himself.

"It seems like the last generation's hero also stood up against the Demon Lord, but the situation then was completely different to what it is now," I said.

From the parts of the notebook that I could still read, the old Demon Lord's army got up to some really horrendous stuff. Unlike now, when they simply threw themselves at us in a full-frontal assault, back then they launched surprise attacks and assaults from blind spots. They also captured humans to use as sources of magic power and brainwashed people.

"Whoa," I uttered. "It wasn't just villages but whole nations that betrayed the hero. That's unbearably unfair."

Were the old Demon Lord and the present Demon Lord really the same person? Based on this book, the difference felt like night and day.

Through it all, however, and no matter the schemes, the hero overcame it all. All the stories on their own were like the legend of a great hero, but there was no joy in the way the notebook told its story—if anything, it felt like a tragedy. It was as if the author pitied the hero.

"Things were so rough back then . . ." I muttered.

As someone living in the present, there wasn't much more I could do than feel sympathetic. Even though I understood them, I couldn't change the circumstances he was in.

"The demi-humans, they adored the hero," I said.

"That's what it seems like," replied Amako, "but I don't know much about it. Back at home, my people hate humans, but I've never heard anyone say that they hate the hero. For us beastkin, the hero is considered someone truly special, even now."

I took another look through the notebook. I couldn't tell from this alone what the hero had done for demi-humans, but perhaps it was something so great that they revered him for it.

"Hm?"

That was when I noticed a small note stuck in between pages of the notebook. There was a hand-drawn illustration. There was some text, too, but I could barely read it.

"Is it an alligator? Or maybe a lizard? Oh, wait. It's got wings," I said.

The creature on the note had a wide mouth that stretched as far as its cheeks, and flames spewed from its mouth. Wings sprouted from its back as sharp as blades. It wasn't a particularly well-drawn image, but it was creepy all the same. The note stuck in the page was written by someone else—probably Nea who had deciphered the text.

There was nothing else you could call it but a calamity. Its breath rotted anything and everything. Its claws split the earth, and its tail leveled mountains.

It was a monster, a dragon of pure evil.

When it passed through forests, the greenery eroded, and all living creatures were devoured. When it passed through nations, the water went putrid, and all the citizens were killed without reason.

The black dragon committed any and all atrocities for the sheer joy of it.

However, the creature was felled by the hero. Their battleground was Samariarl. The dragon had appeared before the hero, and with its destruction and poison seeping into ground, it attacked him.

The notebook describes the hero's magical power as absolute, but even his powerful spells were useless against the dragon's thick scales. Their battle was waged for a full three days and nights.

I did not get to see it myself, but I did get to see the hero land the finishing blow. He leaped into the dragon's mouth and plunged his short sword into the beast's heart with everything he had, killing it. Although, to use the hero's words, he merely "locked it away".

According to the man himself, he said he could not, at present, completely slay the dragon. Even with its heart pierced, and even when it was no longer breathing, the dragon would not fully disappear. The particles of what it was would remain in its body, where it would continue to exist. A truly horrifying thought.

Is it that the dragon is a truly dangerous creature, as the hero himself said? Or is it that the hero himself is on an entirely different plain of existence, having contained the dragon's powers? I cannot tell.

In the center of their battleground, strewn with debris, I stood staring up at the lifeless dragon. I felt a sudden whisper of fear in my heart—a foolish thought that voiced itself in my mind:

Was it that he **could not** *kill the dragon, or that he simply* **did not** *kill it?*

I mustered enough courage to ask this directly, but the hero gave me nothing in the way of a reply. Even now, I cannot comprehend exactly what his silence conveyed.

A dragon of pure evil.

Now, I knew about dragons from fantasy novels and the like, but I really didn't want one of them turning up right in front of our eyes. Especially considering that, if the notebook was telling the truth, I probably couldn't handle this dragon myself. Against a foe like that, I'd probably need senpai and Kazuki fighting alongside me.

The thought made me realize that the past hero—who took the dragon out alone—really was extraordinary. He was so powerful it was like he was cheating, or he'd hacked the system. It seemed like there was always *someone* like that in stories like this.

"Why did Nea spend so much time on this?" I wondered aloud.

I didn't know her all that well, but I couldn't help wondering why she'd put so much effort into deciphering this particular section of the notebook. Perhaps it just caught her fancy for some reason or another. Perhaps it didn't even matter.

"Usato," said Amako suddenly.

"What's up?"

I closed the notebook and turned to Amako, whose face was clouded with worry.

"You remember that big hall we found in that manor last night?" she asked.

I had to assume she was talking about the third floor where I jumped off the balcony.

"I do," I replied. "What about it?"

"The moment I saw it, it struck me. It felt the same as the place I saw in my dream."

Well, that's going to add an element of anxiety to our rescue plan.

"But it might be different," continued Amako. "In my dream, the room was all busted up . . . but it couldn't see it clearly."

That explained why Amako reacted the way she did when she saw the room. She probably didn't tell me because we were looking for the necromancer at the time and she didn't want to complicate things.

What a weird time to think of being considerate, though.

"Does that mean that Nea is the one who stabs me?" I asked.

"Probably."

Then it's decided. As soon as I see the girl, I'm knocking her out cold with a healing punch.

"I know you said that everything would be fine because you've got healing magic," said Amako, her eyes downcast, "but Nea can use sorcery. If you get cursed . . ."

A curse, huh? I hadn't even really considered the possibility. But when I thought about how easily I fell into Nea's trap yesterday, I could see why Amako was so worried. At the same time, we'd never get anywhere if we let our fear get the better of us. Yeah, some hesitation was a necessity in times of danger, but with Aruku taken prisoner, we had no other choice but to head out there and save him.

"I'm not going to go down because of some curse. You know that, right?" I said with a reassuring smile. "I found my way out of the last one with brute strength, didn't I? You've got nothing to worry about."

"But I *am* worried . . . because you're inhuman. You're the kind of weirdo who doesn't even blink when it comes to doing the type of thing an ordinary person would never think of, but at the same time, you're still kind of a human yourself, too."

"How about I give you a little something to worry about right now?"

I can't believe she can say that kind of thing with such a worried look on her face!

I let out a sigh and leaned back against the sleeping Blurin.

"You're letting your premonitions get the better of you," I said.

"But . . . they're never wrong."

"But you only see them one way," I replied. "Yes, it's true that you see a definite and unshakeable future, but you only see that future from your point of view."

I wasn't telling Amako she was wrong—I just wanted her to know that she didn't have to be so pessimistic.

"You might have seen drops of blood dripping to the floor, but you didn't actually see me get stabbed, right? For all we know, the blood you saw might be from the person who tries to stab me. That same person had their back against the wall and were hidden by my body, so you couldn't see them, yeah? What I'm trying to say is, based on what you've seen, there's a whole range of possibilities for what could happen."

"Really?"

"For starters, a simple short sword attack is something I can dodge. And even if I can't, I'll use my arm against it. I'm confident it'll break."

As long as I could see the sword coming, I'd dodge it. As for whether it was the sword or my arm that would break, I left that part vague. In any case, given my strength and my eyesight, I'd be able to defend myself. I could heal my wounds and my exhaustion with my magic, and I'd be more than able to react even if I was taken off guard—after all, I'd trained to respond to the blistering pace of Rose's fists.

"But Usato, you might get *stabbed*," said Amako.

"That's true. But you just said it yourself. *Might* get stabbed. Not *will* get stabbed. So there's still a ray of hope, right?"

"You . . . call that hope?"

I shot the sulking Amako a smile. I could see why she was worried; I really could. It couldn't be easy being the only one who could see the future.

"Look, you're not alone," I said. "You don't have to carry your burden all by yourself."

Amako looked up at me, surprise flashing across her face.

"Huh . . .?" she uttered.

I could tell by the way Amako talked that the future she saw was not always the future she wanted. It was also unwavering, which brought about a sense of powerlessness. I could only imagine how it felt for her, wrapped up in that feeling back when she was in the Llinger Kingdom.

But she wasn't alone anymore. She had us.

"Trust me," I said, "just like I trust you."

"You mean . . . it's really going to be okay?"

"Of course."

I admit I felt a tinge of regret for saying something so embarrassing out loud, but Amako simply nodded.

"Okay then," she said. "Then I'll try to trust you . . . more."

I liked what I heard, and I nodded.

Just then, Amako stood up with a serious look on her face.

"When we go to rescue Aruku, let's . . . do that thing you suggested."

"Uh . . . that thing?"

"Ugh. It was *your* idea! How did you forget?"

I felt like I'd lost Amako's trust in a single instant. With her icy cold gaze locked on me, I crossed my arms and dropped into thought. What did she mean by "that thing"? It must have been some kind of strategy or tactic.

"You mean a diversion?" I asked.

"No! I mean me . . . and you . . . together . . ."

Amako's cheeks flushed red. Her lips twisted into an awkward cringe. But, finally, I understood what she was trying to say. She was talking about the unstoppable combo idea I'd brought up before we left for the manor.

"Aha," I said. "*That* thing. You realize I said that as a joke, right?"

The disappointment in Amako's face was loud and clear.

"That was a *joke*?"

I'd said it as a joke, but conceptually it really *was* the ultimate combo. But, in order for the whole thing to work, Amako had to be on board with it.

"It *was*. But now things are different. After what happened yesterday, it's not a bad strategy at all. That is, if you're okay with it."

"I want to save Aruku," said Amako. "And also . . . I made up my mind to trust you."

"Awesome."

We were all set. With Amako and I working in tandem, we'd get to Nea in no time flat. We also had Blurin with us now. I'd be making sure his claws went to work.

The plan was set. We'd put it into action that very night.

The only thing left to worry about was how Nea would approach us now that she knew all about us.

* * *

"Hm? Where is it?"

I went through all the books in the study, but I couldn't find it. I knew that Usato and Amako had been here last night . . . when I checked to make sure that everything was where it was supposed to be, I realized that a notebook had gone missing.

Casting that hex to bind Usato had exhausted me. I was so depleted of magic power that I collapsed and fell sleep. Because of that, I'd forgotten to turn the lights off in the study before I left.

"I just never thought things would be this much trouble," I muttered.

I poked my head up from all the books, tidied my messy hair, and gave up on looking for the notebook.

"Damn it, there are so few remaining records of the hero," I said to myself. "Is it possible that they took the notebook? But to any ordinary human, it's no different from any other worn-out old notebook. Ugh. There are still things I wanted to research in that book!"

I sat back in my comfy and well-used chair and dropped into thought.

Why would Usato and the girl take the notebook?

"Were they just curious? Was it the girl? They could have

sold the sorcery books for a good price, but they didn't take those. Instead, they took the notebook. It's not even clear that the thing has any historical value on the face of it."

Or was there, perhaps, something specific about the notebook that drew Usato's interest? The hero was revered by the people, after all.

The hero had stood against the Demon Lord and his forces all on his own. I'd heard that some nations worshiped him fanatically, but I knew that the Llinger Kingdom was not among them.

"He doesn't strike me as the fanatical type," I mused. "I don't think that would interest him. The girl, Amako? Maybe. I can't tell what that girl is thinking."

She was unlike any beastkin I'd met. No ordinary beastkin would want to be around humans.

"Whatever the case, they still took the notebook."

And fortunately for me, I had a way of finding out exactly *why* they took it with them. I leaned back and relaxed against the chair's armrests and spoke to the man behind me.

"What do *you* think?"

There was no response. I looked at Aruku, standing in front of the study door with his blank gaze, and I laughed happily. With Aruku under my control, I could do whatever I wanted with him, and that included learning about where he came from, everything he'd done, and all of his relationships.

I would have preferred talking to him while he was

conscious, but after observing him and the others in the village, I knew that Aruku would never betray his friends—he was too strong of heart for that. He was the type of person other people often liked, but to me, a monster, he was just really annoying.

"Why do you think Usato would be interested in a book about the hero?" I asked, my voice pushing for an answer.

A moment later, Aruku responded in a toneless voice.

"Sir Usato has ties to the heroes."

"Huh?"

Aruku's answer took me completely by surprise. I slid out of my chair in amazement and, in doing so, knocked over a huge pile of books.

*Ties to the heroes? What does **that** mean? That is so **very** intriguing.*

"What do you mean? You're not saying he's an impostor, are you?"

I could hear my own voice trembling as I spoke.

Aruku shook his head. I felt joy and incredulity wash over me. I struggled to keep my growing excitement under control.

"Give me more details . . . oh, wait. Scratch that! Tell me more about Amako."

First, I'd ask about the beastkin, then I'd find out more about Usato. Even after everything I'd learned over two hundred years, I had a feeling that Usato's story was going to overwhelm me. So, I'd start with that unusual beastkin, Amako.

"Miss Amako is a beastkin," started Aruku.

"Yes, yes, I already know *that*. Get to the good stuff."

"She traveled to the Llinger Kingdom in order to save her mother in the Beastlands."

"Oh, her mother, huh?"

My own mother was a long distant memory. She was a necromancer. She'd been killed by humans well before I'd had the chance to know her. The same was true of my father, the vampire. But this wasn't to say that I begrudged humans at all—if anything, my parents were guilty of the kind of evil deeds that invite vengeance.

But that aside, I was a little impressed to hear that Amako had traveled from the Beastlands to Llinger.

But only a little.

"Her magic . . ." uttered Aruku.

"It's a sensory magic, right?" I said.

"It is not. They lied to you about it."

"I treated you all so well, and you still didn't trust me?"

Then again, I was all about deceiving them from the moment we met, so it wasn't like I could talk. But I didn't sense that they knew what I was up to, which meant perhaps they had some other reason to be careful.

"Then what magic *does* Amako wield?" I asked.

"She has a precognitive vision that allows her to see the future."

"You're joking."

But even when I pushed him on it, Aruku's expressionless answer never changed. Precognitive vision was exceptionally rare and only manifested in an extremely small number of beastkin. Anyone with such magic was considered hugely valuable to the citizens of the Beastlands. Beastkin with precognitive vision were called "time readers".

"This is all too much," I muttered.

A person with ties to the heroes and a time reader? What the heck kind of a duo is that? It's not normal, that's for sure. And if the beastkin girl wanted to be with Usato, then what did that make him? There's absolutely no way in the world that he's just an ordinary healer!

"Who are all of you . . . wait. What *is* Usato?" I asked, my voice quivering as I asked a long lingering question. "Is he human?"

"Sir Usato is . . ." said Aruku.

If he really was a person with ties to the hero, then he was *exactly* what I wanted to help me to pass the time here. I had a feeling I knew what was coming, but I listened carefully to Aruku's next words.

"Sir Usato is a human who came here from another world, together with the heroes."

At first, I didn't completely understand what Aruku had just said. But slowly, a potential answer rose to my mind.

"Summoning . . . heroes," I uttered.

It was a transportation magic that allowed for those with heroic qualities to be brought from other worlds. Or, more accurately, a magical ceremony.

That's what Aruku must have been talking about.

"Oh my," I sang.

What a most wonderful and fresh source of information.

Nothing I had ever encountered in my entire life could equal the curiosity that welled in me now. I finally understood exactly why it was that Usato had so stubbornly refused to open up to me, too.

"You were wise to stay silent, Usato," I said. "There is no *way* I am going to let a story like *that* slip through my grasp."

And now that I knew, I was *not* going to let him go. I would keep him here like a treasured artifact. His was an entirely different world to the one that I had lived in for two hundred years—a mystery that I could not even imagine.

At first, I'd merely been curious about him. I'd thought him little more than a potential puppet I could use to help kill some time. But after our first meeting, I'd grown intrigued, and now, I was obsessed.

"Tell me *everything*," I said.

"Very well . . ."

Aruku told me about Usato being summoned with the two heroes. He told me about the rescue team that Usato joined, and the harsh training he endured. He told me about the blue grizzly, Blurin, and their bond of trust that did not include a familiar contract. He told me all about the lives that Usato saved when he joined the battle against the Demon Lord's forces and how Usato had brought down the lynch-pin of the Demon Lord's offense.

The more I heard, the more I wanted him. He was interesting solely for being a person from another world, and yet his adventures since his arrival here were beyond engrossing. I couldn't believe that it had all taken place within a single year.

"You know, I *did* think it was weird, leaving such important letters in the hands of a healer. Even if the healer was strong, it still didn't make sense. But now all the pieces fit. Usato is entirely capable of such a duty!"

He was a hero himself, who had run circles around the Demon Lord's army. He'd been summoned from another world and was far from any ordinary human. Anyone who could become as strong as he had with only healing magic was undoubtedly heroic.

"I. Am. *So.* Going to have him! But the zombies and the villagers won't be nearly enough. Hey, Aruku—does Usato use any special magic?"

"Sir Usato's main weapon is his pure physicality. Healing magic is simply the way he built his body. The only person that could surpass him in terms of physical abilities, as far as I am aware, is his teacher."

"Wow. Now that *is* something!"

I had to admit that when I came back to the manor and found a zombie with its arms and legs completely mangled, I was honestly bewildered. I didn't know what kind of monster would do something so clearly painful to its prey.

But now I knew that it was the work of Usato. And if he could silence a zombie before it could even make a sound, then he'd take out a human opponent in mere seconds.

I knew that I could cast a binding hex like I had the previous evening, but when I thought about everything that happened when we last faced off, I didn't think Usato would fall for the same trick a second time. My sorcery wasn't good for battle, and there was no way I'd be able to compete with such monstrous physical strength head on.

"Seeing as my charms were completely ineffective, I have to assume that his mental strength is just as stupidly strong."

The truth of the matter was I'd never encountered anyone who could resist my charms before. I'd prepared myself for utter embarrassment as I launched into a full hug on the guy, but it honestly surprised me to discover that even then my charm was useless.

All of this left me with a pressing question: just what could I do to capture him?

After some time lost in thought, the answer simply drifted to the forefront of my mind.

"Ah, yes. I'll use *that*."

The manor was still home to one piece of my deceased father's collection. That was the very reason I had been researching the notebook about the hero. I felt eagerly impatient, but I kept the feeling under wraps as I left the study and dashed down the stairs to the door that led to the basement. The light of the sun shone upon it ominously as I threw the door open.

"I never thought I'd use you," I said, "but now I'm up against the kind of monster I'll never catch without you."

I dropped down into the basement and looked up as the sun shone down upon the creature. If zombies and humans and monsters wouldn't do, then perhaps this would...

"Oh yes," I sang.

Its huge body reached up to the ceiling. Its mouth had been ripped open, its right eye had been gouged out, and its wings were cut to pieces. It was a corpse with only one eye and one wing, and it stood silently before me.

The Wrong Way To Use Healing Magic 4

CHAPTER 7

Healing Magic Versus Fire Magic!

When night fell, Blurin and I got to a point halfway between the village and the manor. That was where we started warming up. We had to be ready for a rough night—this was both our assault on Nea and our Aruku rescue mission.

"Blurin," I said. "We'll be surrounded by enemies, both outside the manor and inside of it. Be ready."

The grizzly let out a growl in reply that meant *don't sweat it*.

I was confident Blurin could handle himself. I'd need him in shape—the grizzly would be handling any zombies we found roaming outside of the manor.

"Usato, I found the villagers," said Amako, who'd just come back from a scouting trip.

"What are we looking at?"

Amako's answer here would determine whether we'd be able to go all out.

"Everyone's at the village," she said. "It looks to me like Nea doesn't want to get the villagers involved."

"Which means she plans to take us on with just Aruku and her zombies. I wonder if she thinks that it's enough, or if she's hiding an ace up her sleeve . . . something so strong that she doesn't even *need* to use the villagers as hostages."

Whatever the case, we still had to head out to rescue Aruku, no matter what. And at least with the villagers clear, we could raise hell while we did it.

"Our horse is just fine," said Amako, "and I think all of our baggage is at Tetra's place, just like we left it. Oh, and I brought this."

Amako held out a long strip of cloth. It was frayed in places, which made me think that perhaps it was once a curtain. I took it in hand, and then looked Amako in the eyes.

"You're sure about this?" I asked. "It could get pretty rough out there."

"I want to save Aruku too," she replied. "You can go as crazy as you want—I'm totally used to it now."

There was a strength in Amako's eyes. She had far more grit than the girl who had shrieked when we'd jumped from the third floor balcony the previous evening. I nodded, then turned away from Amako and kneeled down. Amako put her arms around my neck and jumped on my back. Once I was sure that her legs were wrapped around my torso, I stood to my feet.

"This is going to be easier than I thought," I said.

This was our strategy: Amako's precognitive vision combined with my speed and strength. As long as we could work together as a team, we'd be able to overcome almost any attack that was thrown at us.

"Alright, let's get you locked in place," I said.

I used the cloth that Amako had just given me to secure her

against my back. She was light. I wasn't going to have to worry about a heavy load.

"Amako, is it tight or uncomfortable anywhere?" I asked.

"What do you think, Usato?" she asked back.

What do I think? What does that mean? Oh, **now** *I get it.*

"Amako, you've got about three years to go before you have to worry about bust si—gah!"

I felt Amako's arms lock around my neck and start choking me.

"Ngh! Wait!" I spat.

The blood drained from my face as I tapped Amako's arm as a sign of surrender, which seemed to satisfy her.

"I'll put you out next time," she said, releasing her grip.

Amako's voice sent a shiver down my spine.

"Huh? Uh, yes ma'am," I said, my voice quivering as I fought to get my breath back.

What was that? All of a sudden, she wields my own life over me?

The pressure emanating from my back forced me into a cold sweat. I put my attention on Blurin in an attempt to shrug it off.

"Blurin, you good to go?" I asked.

The grizzly's body shook as it roared in the affirmative. Blurin was all set.

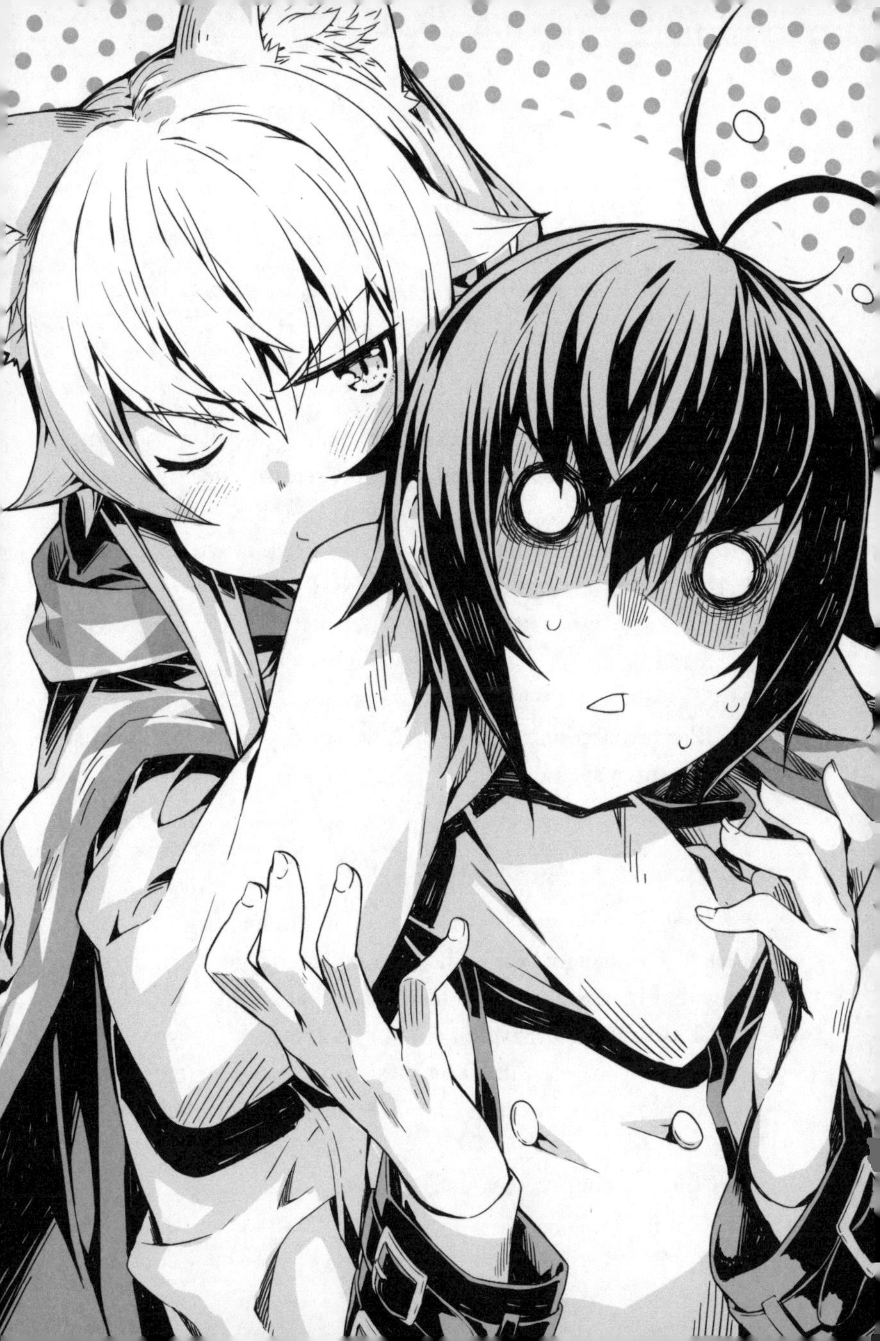

"Amako, you just focus on the future. As long as I'm here, no attack will hit us, and nothing's going to stop us."

"Got it. I trust you."

Then let's do this.

Blurin and I turned toward the manor. The plan was simple—take Nea out hard and fast and release Aruku and the zombies. As for releasing the villagers . . . well, I still had some questions, and I couldn't say for certain whether we could help them. I didn't know why Nea had lived her life as a villager, pretending to be Tetra's daughter, but that didn't matter. First, we would make her give us our friend back.

"Let's get to it!" I shouted.

Blurin roared in reply. I felt Amako's grip on me tighten as I broke into a sprint.

* * *

We came within sight of the outline of the manor in no time at all. The only lights on in the manor were on the third floor. I knew that Nea would be waiting for us there.

"I just *knew* there were going to be zombies!" I said.

Some twenty or thirty zombies surrounded the manor, but they weren't my concern—they'd be facing a different opponent.

"Blurin! They're all yours!"

The grizzly broke out in front of me with a roar, plowing into the zombies that tried to block our path. The impact would have been enough to cause serious injury if it were living creatures we were up against, but zombies would get up and keep on moving even if their bones were crushed and broken.

"You're on your own from here, Blurin!" I shouted.

Amako and I didn't have time to take on each and every zombie, so we left Blurin with the area outside of the manor and burst in through the front doors.

"Don't think we're going to be polite enough to knock, Nea!" I shouted as I kicked down the doors, which surprisingly had been neatly repaired.

The zombies that had been waiting to ambush us were sent flying.

"Three to the right, one to the left, and three on the stairs," said Amako. "You've got this, Usato."

"You bet. Coming through!"

As I listened to Amako's instructions, I sent my fists flying at the four zombies coming our way and launched them right through the manor walls. It was a piece of cake when I knew exactly where they were coming from.

"Head straight up the stairs," said Amako.

As we raced upward, we saw the three zombies Amako had warned me of. I calmly took the arms of the zombie that was reaching out for me and swung it at the other two, knocking them all to the ground and rendering them useless.

"You're all clear to head straight up, Usato," said Amako. "There's nobody in front of the third-floor doors."

I picked up speed and raced upward but stopped right in front of the doors to the hall.

"Usato," said Amako, suddenly confused, "what are you—"

"Just a little something to let Nea know we've arrived," I said, clenching my fists.

The girl takes control of my friend and tries to completely derail our journey? Of course, I'm going to be mad.

"You wanted us! You got us!" I bellowed. "You damned vampire shut-in!"

Then I launched my fist at the doors, which practically exploded because I wasn't holding back in the slightest.

"So, you're finally here," said Nea, looking like the picture of calm until she realized a door was flying directly at her. "What the?! Are you crazy?!"

She quickly dropped to the floor as the flying door collided with one of the hall's windows, leaving a gaping hole behind it.

"Huh? What? What are you doing to my manor?!" Nea cried. "Do you have any idea how hard this place is to mend?! How about considering *that* before you make your entrance?!"

"Like I even give a damn!" I retorted. "I don't have time to care about the state of your manor! Now stay still while I knock you unconscious."

"Eek!"

I ignored everything Nea said and launched at her. I was going to smack her in the head with a chop and put her straight out.

"Usato!" cried Amako, stopping me before I could close in completely.

Just at that moment, I felt something approaching at rapid speed, and leaped away from Nea. As I did so, a sword swung down right where I'd been standing. Attached to the dull, glimmering sword was a suit of heavy armor, and inside of it stood Aruku, his empty gaze glaring at us while Nea fought to get her breath back. He was protecting her.

"Jeez, that was a close one," Nea muttered before bursting into giggles. "Well, looks like the tables have turned, don't you think?"

She wore a supremely satisfied expression while she slid in behind her bodyguard and flashed us a daring grin. When I tried to move to find an opening, Aruku moved to block me.

Can't afford to be careless.

"I guess you're not going to let us through, huh, Aruku?" I asked.

No response. Even under her control, he was intent on defending what he was ordered to protect. For many long years, he had stood at the Llinger castle gates. I knew that getting by him was going to be anything but a simple task.

"Well, this sucks," I muttered.

I heaved a great sigh and let my hands drop to my sides. I knew I wasn't going to land anything on Nea now. Relief filled her face the moment she saw it happen, but her head tilted in confusion when she saw Amako strapped to my back.

"What is going on with the two of you . . .? Oh, that's so she can focus on her magic, right?"

"So you *did* talk to Aruku."

"Of course. And I know *all* about you too, Usato."

It was exactly what I'd feared—Nea knew everything.

I just hope I can somehow take her out before things get any more troublesome.

"So I hear you came from another world?" asked Nea.

"Yep. I wasn't born or raised here. I really didn't want you to find out, but there's nothing I can do about it now."

I just had to man up and face things head on—that meant knocking out Aruku before I turned my attention to Nea.

"Amako, sorry, but . . . I'm going to need you to get down."

"Got it."

In a relatively confined space like this hall, fighting wouldn't be easy for me with Amako on my back. There was also the fact that I didn't know the true extent of Aruku's fire magic abilities.

"Out of the frying pan, into the fire," I muttered.

The first thing that sprang to mind when I thought of fire magic was the fight in Luqvist between Nack and Mina, and her burst magic. If Aruku was to fire off anything with that kind of wide strike range, I didn't think Amako would get out of it unscathed, let alone me.

I let Amako down then raised my fists. Aruku stood silently with his sword at the ready.

"As you've probably guessed, I'm not going to hold back in the slightest," said Nea. "I've heard all about your power, your durability, and all of your escapades. Aruku told me *everything*. So he's going to fight you with everything he's got. *And* I gave him a little help!"

"A little help?"

What in the world did Nea do to him? Or does she mean that ugly armor she put him in?

As far as I could tell, outside of his empty gaze and that set of armor, Aruku didn't look any different.

So I guess the only way to find out is in the thick of things.

"Attack!" Nea shouted.

Aruku dropped his hips slightly at the sound of Nea's voice, then sprang at me in a flash. His sword was covered in flames. I knew that he could easily slice almost anything in two given how sharp his blade was. Aruku launched a strike from up high, but I leaped backward as it came down at me. I jumped to safety as I wrapped my hands in healing magic.

"Ow! That's hot!" I cried.

My healing magic was no use against zombies, but against

a living opponent? That was a different story. I'd knock Aruku unconscious with a healing punch.

"I've got no other choice!" I spat.

But in order to land that punch, I had to evade Aruku's sword and get in close enough to hit him. When I'd fought Halpha back in Luqvist, I'd been able to defend directly against his strikes because he fought me with a staff. Against a blade like this, however, any strike would cut right through me. This made things entirely different. The smallest of mistakes could cost me my life.

Just then, Aruku's sword rose in an upward strike, almost brushing the tip of my nose. The heat of the fire caused me to break into a sweat.

"Whoa!" I cried, leaping backward. "If that hits me, we're talking about more than just a simple burn!"

I knew that Nea wasn't out to kill me, but it was pretty clear that anything less than that was fair game.

I can't let this fight go on for too long . . .

"Sorry Aruku, but I'm going to have to hit you!"

I clenched my fist tight as Aruku swung a horizontal strike at me, then rushed in after it. I held out my right hand to block Aruku's own right hand—which was wielding his sword—and as soon as I was in range, I launched a healing punch with my left hand straight at his chest.

The Wrong Way To Use Healing Magic 4

"There!" I shouted.

I felt the impact of the punch in my hand. Even if he didn't go out cold, I'd hit him hard enough to send him reeling to the floor. With him out of the game, all I'd have to deal with was Nea. That's what I was thinking about when I suddenly noticed the strange magical seal appear where I'd hit Aruku in the chest.

"What the?!"

It looked awfully similar to the patterns I'd seen when I was bound. It flickered from Aruku's chest to his feet, as if taking the impact of my blow and causing it to flow elsewhere.

"You must be kidding!" I said.

But Aruku was not going to let my moment of confusion go to waste. He placed his left hand on my stomach.

Did I walk straight into his trap?!

But by the time the thought hit me, it was already too late. I panicked to cover my whole body in healing magic just as Aruku launched a fireball from the palm of his hand. A tremendous force ran straight through my body, and I was sent flying straight into a decorative set of armor.

"Usato!" cried Amako.

She was just about to run over to me when I put up a hand to stop her.

"It's alright, I'm okay. Don't worry," I said, rising to my feet.

I let out a breath as I looked down at where I'd been hit.

My rescue team uniform was black and dirtied, but there was no hole in it, and I was otherwise fine. Unlike the flaming sword, perhaps the whole point of Aruku's fireball was to launch his enemy.

"Can't believe my punch didn't work . . ." I muttered.

"Um, why are you almost completely fine?" asked Nea, her face utterly incredulous. "You just took a fireball at point-blank range, didn't you?"

"It's all thanks to my training," I said, brushing the grime off my coat.

"Wait, wait, wait. That doesn't make *any* sense . . ."

Compared to Rose's fist, the impact of that fireball was nothing.

But what is up with that armor Aruku is wearing?

I knew for certain that it wasn't an ability that Aruku had himself. I also knew that it wasn't vampiric or necromantic, either. That meant only one thing.

"It's another type of sorcery," I said.

"Bingo!" Nea cried, giving me a thumbs up.

It was almost like she was overjoyed that I'd realized. There was something so innocent and naive about her expression in that moment—to be on the other end of it was, to be honest, terrifying.

"The armor Aruku is wearing is imbued with my own unique resistance hex, which redirects the force of any blunt-force attacks on it. It's a direct counter to your physical abilities."

So Aruku is resistant to my punches?

Nea loved seeing the confused look on my face, and it spurred her to continue.

"But it *does* have weak points," she said. "It's only resistant to one type of attack, and it's only effective for Aruku. I'll tell you, though, that I feel really bad for it as far as hexes go—it's not particularly convenient, and there are so few situations where it comes in truly handy."

Not convenient, huh?

"You're awfully happy to share the ins and outs of your hexes," I said.

"Well, I mean, wouldn't you just hate to lose to me not knowing how I won?"

The way she said that really ticks me off . . .

Still, the truth of the matter was that the hex on Aruku was a really bad match-up for me. If the force of all my kicks and punches was redirected, I was pretty much all out of options. Nea must have read my thoughts, because her lips twisted into a smile, and she giggled.

"If you want to take Aruku out of the picture, you can always use one of those swords or axes, you know? Or . . . maybe you could use some kind of attack magic! Well, that's if you don't mind killing the guy!"

Nea burst into laughter. She was basically telling me to kill him because my physical attacks were pointless. But that wasn't an option. She *knew* that I didn't have any attack magic, but maybe she was bringing it up because she didn't like the way I'd kicked things off.

But her smile was *really* rubbing me the wrong way.

"I guess I'm all out of options then," I said.

"How about giving up? That's what I recommend. I've got an ace up my sleeve even if you happen to get past Aruku. In other words, no matter how much you struggle, my victory is a certainty."

Giving up, huh?

I thought about the words for a few moments, and a derisive grin spread across my face.

"Don't you dare talk down to me, you little wench," I said.

"Huh?!"

"I am *not* going to abandon Aruku, and I am *not* going to give up. You think just because my fists and feet are out of the game that I'm going to throw in the towel?"

I took a pair of steel gauntlets from the armor cluttered at my feet and put them on. They wouldn't last too long, but they'd still let me block some of Aruku's strikes.

"You might think you know me, but all you got was raw data," I said, running a hand through my hair and glaring at Nea. "You don't know anything about the experience I've gained since arriving in this world, or what the rescue team taught me."

"Well, duh, that's the whole reason I'm trying to catch you."

"So you can force it out of me? That's only if you succeed. But let me tell you something you *don't* know—I'm as sore a loser as they come, and I *don't* give up."

It was time to see if I could take a sword head on.

"One small mistake and it all comes crashing down, Usato," I muttered to myself.

I bumped the gauntlets together to test their strength, took a deep breath, then settled into my fighting stance. Aruku stood across from me, his sword pointed at my eyes. My striking attacks were ineffective, but weapons still worked. I *did* have the option of stopping Aruku with a near-fatal blow, but that was far too dangerous—we were here to save him, after all.

"Then we'll just have to go a different route," I muttered.

I didn't have any ideas yet, so I'd just have to find one in the midst of battle. That meant getting up close and personal, where my attacks would land—I'd dodge, I'd parry with my gauntlets, and I'd open up a path for myself.

I stepped forward with my right hand out in front of me and my left cocked at my waist. I had my right leg a half step in front of me so that I'd be ready to move in an instant. It didn't matter what Aruku tried—I'd be ready for it.

"Bring it on!" I shouted.

Aruku rushed at me, his sword ready at his waist, and launched a vertical strike straight down at me. I kept my eyes on it the whole time and used my right gauntlet to knock it slightly of course. I noticed a hint of surprise flash across Aruku's emotionless face.

"Too slow!" I said. "You won't hit me with an attack like that, Aruku!"

But on the inside, I was terrified. Having to fight at close quarters with a flaming sword wasn't exactly a walk in the park. At the same time, however, there was nobody else but me who could save Aruku.

For him—and for all of us—I refused to back down.

Aruku sliced horizontally, and I ducked as the sword whizzed over my head.

"My turn!" I shouted.

I leaped back into striking range and pulled Aruku's shoulder straight into my flying knee. I knew it was a strong attack, but it had zero effect on Aruku's armor. Even keeping him in place as I hit him was no use.

"Whoa!"

I noticed the magic power building in Aruku's hand and leaped out of range. I'd escaped one fireball already, but even *I* wouldn't be unharmed if I caught one of those in the face. Before I could get back to my feet, however, Aruku launched himself into yet another attack.

"Not even going to give me a chance to rest, huh?"

Flames flickered from behind Aruku's sword as he swung

it over and over again in an attempt to get me. I dodged what I could dodge. I parried what I couldn't. But with each strike I felt my breath growing ragged and a stabbing pain in my skin.

"Ugh, so hot . . ."

I parried another strike, this one coming as Aruku spun and let his body weight carry his sword on a diagonal line. He followed it up with a stab, which I bent backward to dodge. It was attack after attack,. I had to parry almost all of them with my gauntlets.

"Ouch!"

I looked down and saw that my right gauntlet was quickly growing red. So, in a panic, I threw it to the ground—it was either going to break, or it was going to leave me horribly burned.

"Damned fire . . ." I said, struggling for breath, "such a pain in the ass."

Nack sure had guts to face off against Mina like that.

I blew on my right arm while I parried a strike with my left. But at that moment, I noticed a slight tremble in Aruku's arm and something stiff in his movements.

"Hm?" I uttered.

As I watched him more carefully, I put together a hypothesis.

"Is he exhausted . . .?"

Nobody could avoid getting tired. My own limits were a little further than normal, but any ordinary human would feel the effects of moving without rest. On top of that, while I was focused on defense, Aruku was attacking non-stop. This would have tired him out more than me.

Usually, at this point in the battle, you'd try to make some distance and catch your breath. But Aruku was under Nea's control. He would not stop swinging his sword until he had accomplished the orders that she had given him.

"If he wasn't under her control..."

Under normal circumstances, Aruku never would have let himself get pulled into a battle of endurance. He wouldn't have bothered with something as down and dirty as a close-quarters fight. He would have made the battle more technical, where I was weakest and where he could take advantage of me.

I dodged another one of Aruku's strikes and glanced at Nea.

"Do it!" she shouted. "Get him! Yes, like that!"

She was very excited. Seeing me stuck on defense made her even more assured of her own victory. But seeing her like that told me she wasn't very experienced when it came to battle. The whole reason she'd cowered in fear when I attempted my first strike was because she knew that I could easily take her down if I got close enough. I had to get to her and knock her out before Aruku's body broke completely. Unfortunately, Aruku wasn't going to make it easy on me.

If only there was some other way to attack Nea...

And then it hit me. I just had to flip my perspective.

"I've got it!" I shouted.

If close-quarter attacks weren't effective, I'd have to use another method.

"I've got just the thing!" again I exclaimed.

I turned my focus back on Aruku and took a big step right into close range. If I tried to hit him here, I'd simply be repeating the same mistake again, but now I had a different idea. This time I didn't hit Aruku straight on, but instead knocked Aruku upward with my fists. The force and shock of my blows were ineffective, but that didn't mean I couldn't lift the guy up into the air!

And Aruku's body proved my point. It flew up from the floor. I felt the smile growing on my face as I turned to look at Nea.

"Here we go! Prepare yourself, Nea!" I shouted.

"Eek! What?! Why me?!" cried Nea in utter shock.

I glared straight at her as I took a hold of Aruku midair and launched him straight toward Nea, who was standing by the windows. I already knew that with a hex on his armor, Aruku would be fine. But what about the person he collided with? How would she fare?

"What?! Huh?! You're aiming for *me*?!"

Aruku flew toward Nea, who was frozen in place.

"Aruku! Stop!" she screamed.

Right before Aruku collided with her, he dug his sword

down and stabbed it into the floor. The sound of his armor impacting the ground echoed around us. The fall certainly didn't look like it felt good.

"Damn it," I spat. "He stopped."

"What the heck?! Are you crazy?! All the things you could have done, and you launch your friend straight at me!"

Did she just call me crazy? Well, whatever. I'll throw him as many times as I have to.

I readied myself as Aruku lifted himself from the ground with a groan.

"Ugh . . ." he uttered.

"Huh?"

*He's hurt. But it wasn't because I hit him. It must have been the weight of the armor and his own body when he fell. Does that mean he's not impervious to **every** kind of impact?*

"I think I get it," I said.

I felt like I was getting a better feel for how Nea's resistance hex worked.

"So your resistance hex is only resistant to striking attacks, then. Well, that makes things simple. I'll just throw him at you until he's unconscious."

"This is your friend you're talking about, right? And you're just going to beat him into submission . . .? Um, are you even capable of that?"

I heard that fear slip into your voice, Nea.

In reply, I nodded and raised my fists.

"I'll do what I have to do," I said. "One reason I was so focused on defense was to ensure that Aruku didn't cut me or Amako. I don't want him to have to carry around any guilt from hurting us, so I'm going to stop him."

Nea flinched at my words.

"I can't believe it," she said. "You leave me no choice."

She put a hand on Aruku and murmured something. I glanced at Amako, but she shook her head—even her beastkin ears couldn't pick up what Nea said.

"It really would have been much better for you if you'd let things end here," said Nea.

"What does that mean?" I asked.

But before she could answer, Aruku was on the move. He'd had a chance to catch his breath, but his movements were still slow.

It doesn't matter what she has planned. I'll just do what I did the last time and . . . huh?!

"What the?!"

A huge fireball flew toward me. I couldn't believe the amount of fire I was seeing in the manor, so I launched a healing bullet in a panic, which collided head on with the fireball and neutralized it.

"What was *that*?" I asked.

Until now the fire magic had been contained to close range,

but now Aruku was happy to throw it around more haphazardly.

"Is it just a distraction? A smoke screen?"

I was surrounded by smoke from the fireball, I was trying to stay ready for Aruku's next attack. Then something was thrust toward my neck. I tried to parry it with my left hand, but I was taken by surprise. It wasn't Aruku's sword coming for me, it was his hand, and it grabbed my own.

"Aruku?!" I shouted.

Suddenly, I was being pulled and swung with tremendous force. My legs left the ground, and I was completely at Aruku's mercy.

"Whoa!"

And just like that, I was thrown straight out of the third floor. I looked down and saw Blurin astride a motionless zombie, slapping it.

"What is that grizzly doing?!"

I could see the impact coming as I fell, so I spun myself and landed on my feet. I saw that Blurin noticed me and was moving in, but then it struck me that Amako was still up there.

"Amako . . ." I uttered.

I turned around to look up and say something, but at that moment, Aruku gripped the railing of the balcony and leaped straight over it.

"I can't see her from here," I said.

I knew that Amako was tougher than she looked, and that

she'd be okay, but I was worried all the same.

Should I ignore Aruku and head back up to help her? No, Blurin can't fight Aruku on his own, and he might even be killed.

"Blurin, you've done enough down there. Head to Amako, now!"

The bear's growl sounded like he was confused.

"You have to look after her!"

The bear roared as if it understood exactly what I'd said, then launched itself inside the manor. Now I knew for sure that Amako would be safe. The problem now was Aruku.

Nea was sitting on the edge of the manor roof, looking down at us.

"I don't have the faintest idea what you're trying to do!" I shouted.

She giggled. Her palm was pointed toward the ground. It was illuminated by a purple light.

"I never believed that a three-story fall would be enough to finish you," she said. "I just wanted to give Aruku a little more space to work with—somewhere he can really flex his powers."

In the next instant, Aruku's sword practically erupted with the most flame I'd seen until now. It had been a silent red when we were in the manor, but now it was brilliantly aflame. I could feel the heat even from a distance.

"Aruku doesn't like using his magic like this. The idea of turning his foes to ashes isn't really in his nature. That's what he said, anyway. But do be careful—that sword is extremely hot, and you're looking at more than simple burns."

Nea chuckled. But where Aruku stood with his flaming sword, I saw Mina. He had sheer power, range, and scope, but it was strange for us to be in here like this—me the healer and Aruku the fire wielder.

"It's like a repeat of Nack versus Mina all over again," I muttered.

Nack had swallowed his fear and he'd stepped up—he'd faced Mina head on. When I thought back to the fight, I couldn't help but smile.

"And I guess as Nack's teacher I, too, have to overcome my own trial by fire."

I also now had a read on how to counter the resistance hex that Nea had cast. Even though kicks and punches didn't work, I still had options. On top of that, moving our fight outside was a horrible tactical decision on Nea's part.

"When you were thinking up your plan," I said, "Aruku had to have warned you about letting me fight in an open space. He had to have told you to keep me in a confined area."

"Yeah, so what? All you can do is kick and punch stuff. Out here in the open Aruku's got the advantage thanks to his explosive fire magic."

"So, you heard him, but you didn't understand him, huh?"

I was trained by Rose herself. Don't you dare doubt me or the rescue team. I wasn't built for kicking and punching. I was built for **running.**

Out here I didn't have to worry about accidentally putting my foot through the floor, and I didn't have to worry at all about Amako getting pulled into things.

"I'm here to save you Aruku!" I said.

"Slice him to pieces!" ordered Nea.

At Nea's command, Aruku brought his flaming sword around in a slicing attack. It was a wave of flame spewing out toward me. I got a short run up and launched off the ground with everything I had, leaping over it.

"No ceilings here and no walls," I shouted.

The moment I landed, I cut to the side, closing in on Aruku from an angle. However, Nea could still see me from above and could also issue orders. Aruku quickly cast a fire wall and kept me from approaching.

"Then I just have to go faster!" I said.

I spun in the opposite direction and kicked off the ground as I picked up the pace. Aruku's fireballs weren't even close to touching me. He was following Nea's orders precisely, but he was still at a clear disadvantage against me.

"You're slow . . . way too slow!"

Aruku was like a robot spamming the same attack over and over again. That wasn't going to be enough. Just like with Mina, the best way to get me would be to use explosive magic to lure me into the perfect position to catch me in one fell swoop. But Aruku couldn't do that while he was under Nea's control.

Nea could throw around Aruku's power all she wanted, but she could not access his true potential!

"Here I come!" I said, changing direction in an instant and facing Aruku.

Nea immediately lost sight of me. Aruku faced where he thought I would be. I moved in quickly. This was my chance to take him down before he realized where I was. But just as I was about to get my hands on him, Aruku turned, his lifeless eyes locked on to me.

Did he notice me? No, he's reacting instinctively?!

As Aruku spun, his sword came down from above in a diagonal arc. I watched the sword and for an instant, I hesitated.

Should I fall back or push through?

My decision was already made, I lifted my left arm to intercept Aruku's sword as I readied my right.

"It's all or nothing!" I shouted.

Rose was the kind of monster who could break a steel sword with her bare hands.

"And if she can do it, then I can too!"

Aruku's sword came down to slice my head in two. I swung my body around and used my left gauntlet to block it. Sparks exploded between us from the impact. I roared as the flaming sword turned the gauntlet red. I fought to endure the flames that threatened to engulf me and refused to back down.

"Break, damn it!" I shouted.

I heard the base of Aruku's sword fracture. I felt it and I swung straight through it. The blade of the flaming sword then broke completely from the hilt with a crack and plunged into the ground still aflame.

But I wasn't done yet.

"This is going to hurt, Aruku!"

I took a step closer to Aruku and took a hold of his wrist and collar. This was my way of working around Nea's resistance hex. If striking was completely nullified, then I'd just have to throw him.

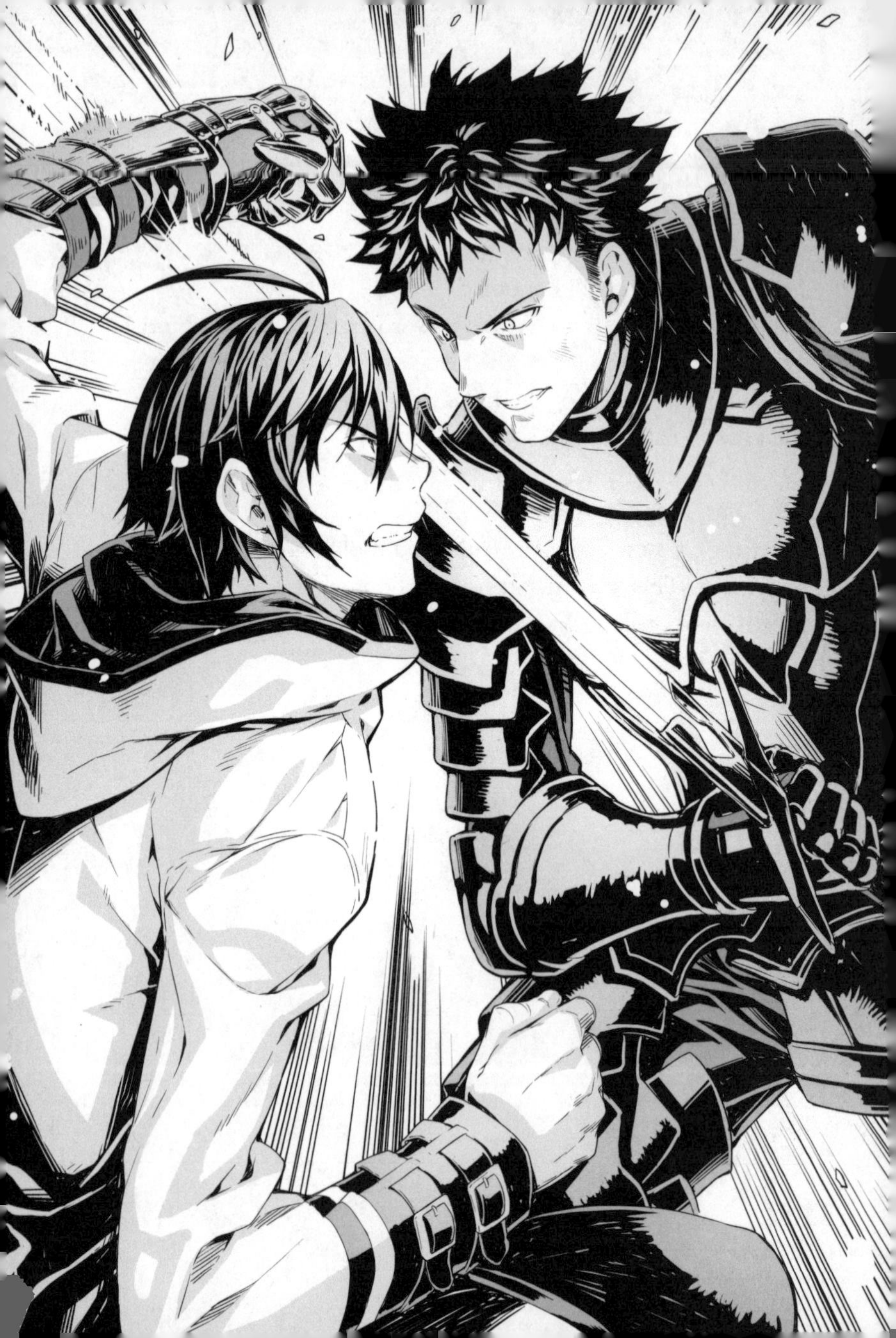

"Hup!" I grunted.

"Wha?!" uttered the stunned Aruku.

This wasn't any fancy judo or aikido technique—this was just me lifting Aruku with everything I had and letting all of that momentum slam him into the ground!

The ground bowed where Aruku hit it, and his armor rattled loudly from the force of the impact. When I heard his despondent groan, I felt bad for what I'd done but immediately healed the damage from my throw attack as I confirmed that he was finally unconscious. I'd been careful to make sure that Aruku didn't land on his head, but I'd nonetheless thrown him with tremendous force to make sure he wasn't going to be able to get back up.

I let out a sigh of relief as I stood back to my feet and caught my breath.

The healing punch healed with each blow, but this time the ability healed at the moment he was thrown to the ground.

"I hereby call it . . . the healing throw!" I stated.

I came up with it in the heat of the moment, but I had a feeling the technique would come in really handy in the future.

In any case, I finally had Aruku unconscious. He probably wasn't free from Nea's brainwashing yet, but I hoped that knocking her out cold would solve that problem.

"Alrighty then," I said, shedding the gauntlet on my left hand.

I healed the burns across my hand and looked up at Nea. Even with Aruku completely out of the game, she didn't look fazed in the slightest. In fact, she looked down at me like she had expected this from the very beginning. It sent a shiver down my spine.

"It's just you now," I said.

"Or is it?" replied Nea.

"I don't care how many more zombies you've got, they won't stop me."

"No match for you, huh? Well, that is, if they're an ordinary zombie, I guess. If they're just a run-of-the-mill, everyday zombie."

I didn't like her tone of voice.

"What are you scheming?" I asked.

Nea simply giggled and shot me a bold grin. She wasn't going to tell me anymore, so I figured there was no better time to knock her out cold.

Then I felt something strange.

Why does she still have her palm pointed at the ground like that?

It didn't look like a sorcery hex. Was she casting something at the ground?

*No, it looks like she's casting **through** the ground.*

"Trying to raise more zombies?" I asked.

She knew just as well as I did that I would crush any ordinary zombie. Did that mean she was raising something like Blurin? A powerful monster zombie?

But there couldn't possibly be any monster corpses . . . Wait. No way.

"The thing that Amako saw . . . in the basement."

The one place I hadn't seen myself. The place that Amako had been strangely terrified of. Just as the thought hit me, the manor shook as terrible sounds echoed from within. The sound of things breaking.

"What the heck?!" I exclaimed as I turned to see what was going on.

It was the sound of something forcing its way to the surface from below the manor. I could see the manor creaking and shaking as it happened.

What is going on?

I watched dumbfounded as a blue shape emerged from the manor and dashed toward me. It was Amako astride Blurin.

"Usato!" she shouted.

"Amako! Blurin! You're safe!" I said. "But what's happening, Amako?"

Amako hopped down from Blurin as she spoke.

"I don't even want to imagine it, but I think the creature I saw in the basement is . . . waking up."

"Can you cut the dramatics and give it to me straight?"

I knew that something bad was happening—that was a certainty—but I still didn't know exactly what. Amako's face went white as a sheet as she turned back to the manor and spoke.

"It's a monster. It's big and it's got a mouth full of sharp teeth, and . . . its one remaining eye is overflowing with pure hatred. I think it's . . ."

Before she could finish, a huge claw burst up through the first floor of the manor. Another soon followed, opening a huge hole.

Even with her own manor being destroyed before her very eyes, Nea cackled with laughter as her wings kept her floating in the air above us. I turned away from the monstrosity that was appearing before us and glared up at her.

"Nea! What did you just wake up?!" I shouted.

"Oh, but isn't that obvious? It's the creature that's going to take you down!"

You want me so bad that you're going to bring something like **this** *back to life?*

I heard a raspy growl from within the manor, and the hairs on my neck stood up. There was a brief moment of silence, and then, the manor floor burst into a cloud of dirt and dust. From it emerged a monster.

"You have to be kidding . . ." I muttered.

It had huge front legs, a single wing on its back, and one ominous, menacing black eye. I was hit hard by the rotting stench of it.

"What *is* that?"

I couldn't believe what I was looking at. It couldn't have been a living creature. Such a creature never should have been allowed to even exist. Its presence alone radiated with hatred and enmity. It opened its mouth and let out a rumble that grew into a deafening roar. It must have reached as far as the heavens.

It was the dragon from the notebook I'd read.

EXTRA

The Start of the Ordeal

"As of tomorrow, you will serve under the Demon Lord as his maid."

So said the chief servant, to me, a girl who was, it must be said, far too inexperienced. The responsibility was far too heavy. I was an ordinary demon who had dared to dream of escaping the countryside for life in the city, and as if out of nowhere, I had received these orders.

Through a haze in which I felt like my own legs were giving out underneath me, I trudged forth toward my new place of work. The life I had been given would now be offered in servitude to the Demon Lord, who had risen from a slumber of hundreds of years. My one salvation was the fact that I would not be alone—I would be working in shifts, sharing the work with the chief maid. However, even in this I was to undertake my duties under her cold, emotionless gaze, which came with its own unique discomfort.

To be blunt, I wanted nothing more than to burst into tears.

The Demon Lord was absolute, and his presence was, in and of itself, overwhelming. It was my duty to tend to him, and yet, before I could feel any sort of honor for my position, I felt only terror. My terror was not directed at the Demon Lord as an individual but rather at the idea that I might make some kind of embarrassing error in the presence of one so revered.

I wanted to avoid the ire of such a demon at all costs. I could not stand the idea that he might shun me.

Such was the sheer power in his gaze when we first met.

For some days, I went about my duties with the utmost care. We made small talk, but the Demon Lord's features were emotionless—I could not tell if he was serious or joking. He sometimes disappeared from a room without so much as a word. Working under this silent pressure wore away at my heart and mind, but nevertheless, I did my utmost to carry out my duties. However, when I finally thought that I had become used to serving at the Demon Lord's side, that very confidence shattered like a pane of fragile glass.

On that day, the Demon Lord burst into what sounded very much like laughter. To see him like that—his eyes emotionless but his mouth curled into the shape of a smile—was, to be honest, creepy. It was scary and so incomprehensible to me that I wanted to cry. Nonetheless, I mustered up my courage and I spoke.

"Whatever is the matter, my Lord?" I asked.

He put his hand to his forehead and laughed. When he was finally done, the Demon Lord turned to me.

"I felt the nostalgic energies of an old dragon," he replied.

"Do you mean . . . a *real* dragon?" I asked.

"They exist now, do they not? One, or was it two? How very intriguing. I wonder if this is his handiwork?"

Those who listened attentively to the Demon Lord were drawn to the charm in his every word. And yet, charmed as I was, I had absolutely no idea what he was talking about. In other words, I was utterly clueless as to what he meant.

"Before I was sealed away," said the Demon Lord, "the dragon was handled in much the same way as I was. It was left in surprisingly good condition to boot."

"Oh . . ." I uttered.

"But its power is out of balance. Perhaps it has been awakened by someone," said the Demon Lord, closing his eyes as if to savor and enjoy each word. "I sense its power mixed with impure magic. In any case, the dragon is weakened—it has been resurrected imperfectly."

I was still perplexed at the idea that dragons really existed. Their existence in the present day had yet to even be confirmed.

"I do not completely understand what you are saying, so I apologize if my question is a foolish one," I ventured, "but is a dragon different to other flying beasts, such as wyverns?"

"Dragons are very different to such domesticated creatures. And this evil dragon is one that sits at the top of all living creatures."

"An *evil* dragon?"

"A power of pure calamity and an existence to be detested."

Though there was a severity to the words the Demon Lord spoke, there was also a clear enjoyment in them.

"A very troublesome creature," he continued. "It does not listen to reason. It does not think. It is only capable of responding to its instincts. It was blessed with great wisdom, and yet, it shuns this gift. A foolish thing."

I could not even imagine such a monster. I had not even known that one once existed. It was difficult for me to even believe that such a beast had been awakened and was now on the verge of wreaking havoc again.

"The only thoughts that fill the dragon's head are those of hatred and destruction. I used the beast but once. In that time, it decimated three whole nations in a single night. Do you understand now why such a monster is so dangerous?"

"There is no word for it other than terrifying," I replied.

The ability to level three whole nations in the space of a single evening was beyond monstrous. I had of course heard the stories of the Demon Lord's invasion before his power was sealed, but even he did not utilize such fiercely destructive tactics.

"Using the dragon is easy," said the Demon Lord. "You merely need to provide a target for it. But attempt to control the monster, and it will quickly turn upon you. Even one such as I couldn't kill the dragon outright."

Though left unspoken, the fact that the Demon Lord could

not kill the dragon only served as a reminder of how extraordinary its power was. But if the Demon Lord himself could not handle such a monster, then was it not as much a threat to demons as it was to humans?

"My Lord, is it not dangerous to leave such a creature on the loose?" I asked.

"You need not worry. As I said earlier, it is weakened. It is not nearly as strong as when it was at its peak. It will rot away and decay on its own before I ever need to lift a finger of my own. Such is the nature of decay," said the Demon Lord with a sweeping gesture.

The Demon Lord did not look in the least bit concerned, but he did put a hand to his jaw in thought as he went on.

"However, left to its own devices, the dragon will likely massacre a great many humans. Centuries of being sealed away combined with decay and its already short-tempered nature will have made the dragon's thoughts a very simple thing. It will turn its destructive impulses on those who first sealed it away. If the hero left any descendants, then they will be first on the list. Then it will be the two heroes who were recently summoned . . . and the one who shares a similar scent. All of them will be its targets."

"So it will become . . ." I uttered.

"Yes," said the Demon Lord, reading my mind. "A rampaging beast. It is loyal only to its instincts, as terrifying as it is arrogant. Such a beast has no point in this world. However, it is also true to say that no purer a creature exists. Though I despise the dragon from the depths of my very heart, I will give it praise where praise is due. And that is why it must die. It should have died back when the hero ran his sword through its heart."

"But it was the hero who sealed the dragon away. Was that not because he could not kill it?"

"You speak nonsense. The hero was more than capable of such a feat. It was not that he *could* not, it was that he *did* not."

I did not understand. I felt confusion wash over me. Based on what the Demon Lord had said, I knew the dragon to be a troublesome creature, especially so for humans. And yet, the hero chose to seal the dragon away even though he wielded the power to slay it. Why would one intentionally take this course of action?

The Demon Lord glanced at the hint of confusion that I showed in the tilt of my head and pointed at himself.

"It was no different for me. I was allowed to live, but the methods were different."

"And you mean to say . . . the hero did that?"

"He did. I was sealed away alive, was I not?"

Did that then mean that the hero was even more powerful than the Demon Lord himself? If he did wield such power, was his decision to keep the Demon Lord and the evil dragon alive an act of compassion and generosity? This seemed the most likely reason.

"It would seem the hero was something of a generous individual," I said, testing my thought, but choosing my words carefully.

In my heart, however, I felt that showing such compassion for your foes was foolish. But the Demon Lord surprised me by grinning.

"Generous, you say," he chuckled, as if tasting the word for himself. "I see . . . generous."

"My Lord?"

I was confused by the shaking I saw in the Demon Lord's shoulders. He leaned back in his chair and laughed, then turned to me with a look of joy on his face.

"Your name?" he asked.

"Erm . . . I am Ciel," I replied.

"Well then, Ciel, as of today you are my personal attendant."

"Oh?"

The words felt like they came out of nowhere. I was now the personal attendant of the one who stood at the very peak of the demon world. I froze. It was yet another responsibility that was far too much for me to bear. And yet, the Demon Lord rested his head on his hand, satisfied with himself.

"It is very boring being the Demon Lord," he stated. "Without someone to talk to, I have nothing to do. But you have the most interesting reactions to what I say. Everyone else here is far too pure for their own good."

"You make it sound as though I am impure, my Lord," I said.

"That is exactly what I said."

To be told such a thing so directly irked me, and even if rude, I felt I should speak up for myself.

"Erm, in my defense, I am . . . pure, my Lord."

The Demon Lord merely grinned at my insolence.

"The ones I am talking about are always looking to offer themselves up for punishment, for some reason or another. If that is what you want, shall I punish you too?"

Now I understood. The chief maid and all the other servants revered the Demon Lord. No, the correct term for it was, perhaps, "worshiped".

I do not want this person to shun my very being. I cannot allow for it.

That was the way that all of them thought.

And such was our fear that, at the slightest error, we prostrated ourselves and offered ourselves for punishment. This was what we felt we should do, but it was not how the Demon Lord himself felt about the matter. What I had learned in the few days that I had served him was that he valued the times during which we could engage in conversation.

Certainly, he was not as cold blooded and merciless as we all thought.

"I sympathize," I said.

"That you understand is enough. It is sufficient."

In that moment, I felt that our hearts grew just a touch closer.

I was about to find out that the Demon Lord was far more thoughtful and extraordinary than I had ever imagined.

The Wrong Way To Use Healing Magic 4

Side Story

Nack's Road to Llinger

I realize it has been a long time since I last wrote.

Firstly, I ask only that you read this letter to its end. This is the last piece of correspondence that I will ever send to you as your son. Once you have finished, you can do as you like with the letter. Burn it, tear it to pieces—you are free to do as you will.

I would like to thank you for enrolling me at Luqvist. Whatever your reasons for doing so may have been, it is thanks to you, my parents, that I have come this far. In truth, I cannot put into words the extent to which I have cursed the two of you, but I cursed myself far more for being so very powerless. Nevertheless, I got to where I am because you raised me. So even if your love was but a fleeting, temporary thing, all the same, it gave me life.

For that, you have my gratitude.

Now, as for the intentions of this letter.

I am renouncing my rank as one of the nobility.

I am renouncing the Agares family name and wish now to live my life by the name of Nack, and Nack alone. Though you may read this and assume that I have gone insane, I assure you that I have not. From the very beginning, I lived my life at Luqvist with a fierce desperation, holding in my heart vague hopes of a life far from all of you.

Every single day at Luqvist was, if I am being honest, a most horrible experience. I endured each and every day unable to ask for help, and it was such torment that one might easily call those days my own personal hell.

And yet, it was thanks to those awful days that I was led to a number of precious encounters. One of those encounters was with another healer.

I imagine you chuckling derisively to read such words.

But the truth remains the same—that encounter changed the course of my life. You looked down upon healing, and you called it useless, but I met a healer of incredible strength, and one who only continues to grow more powerful. In him, I found someone to look up to. He sits at such heights that as I am now, I cannot reach him.

Meeting that healer marked the first time I ever wanted to become stronger. For so long, I used my own misfortunes as an excuse to do absolutely nothing, but now I have seen someone whose footsteps I can follow. That healer helped me to stand on my own two feet, and now I want to be just like him.

No more excuses. No more complaints. I have finally found something I want to achieve with such passion that I will stake my life for it.

And that is why I renounce my noble rank. That is why I will go on as simply Nack.

If you want to laugh at me, then go ahead and laugh. I will continue on regardless.

Please forget that I ever existed.

Goodbye Father, goodbye Mother.
Thank you for the twelve years in which you raised me.

And if such a thing is possible, send my sister my regards, and tell her I said goodbye.

* * *

I wrote the letter and sent it home. Everything I wanted to say was in it. I couldn't think of anything else to put in there. Once I was done, I felt like a weight had lifted from my shoulders.

"They'll probably just burn it," I muttered.

I walked the streets of Luqvist, cringing a little to imagine it. I thought of my father and his ballooned sense of pride. I could see his face, red with rage, as he tore up my letter and threw it in the fireplace. I was well aware that what I'd written could easily bring about such a reaction, but I'd sent the letter anyway.

I thought that I had grown used to the sights and sounds of Luqvist but realized now that it had changed since my fight against Mina.

"Was it always so lively?" I mused.

I had spent so much time walking around with my eyes on the ground, avoiding crowded places, that I'd never really noticed it. The city was bright, energetic, and brimming with life. It was like the scenery had changed from black and white to color. I'd changed so much that the whole world seemed to have changed around me. I almost couldn't believe it.

"I feel like I can barely keep up with how much everything is changing," I said to myself.

"Hey, Nack. What's up? You look lost in your own thoughts."

"What?"

The voice came from behind me. I turned to find Kyo standing there with some fruit in hand. He took a bite out of one, then threw me another as he walked over. I panicked to make sure I didn't drop it, then tilted my head, confused.

"What's with the fruit, Kyo?" I asked.

"I got them from the place I work at. Figured I'd give you one."

"Thank you."

I took a bite and walked side by side with Kyo. My mouth filled with a pleasant sweetness and acidity.

"How's things recently?" asked Kyo.

"Huh?"

"I'm asking if anything's changed since your battle."

Changes, huh . . .

"I've noticed way more people looking at me," I said.

It didn't matter if it was in the streets or at school—wherever I went, I felt somebody's eyes on me. Kyo simply nodded.

"Well, yeah, that's kind of unavoidable. Even now it's like you're the center of attention."

That's because we're walking together, Kyo.

To any ordinary passerby, the sight of a human and a beastkin together was totally unusual.

"Yeah, but I'm not so cold-hearted that I'll cut things off with you just because you're drawing all of his attention," I joked.

Kyo grinned and roughly patted me on the head.

"Look at you," he said, "all grown-up and making jokes all of a sudden!"

"Hey! Knock it off!"

His "pats" were more like slaps, realistically, but in their own way they were proof of Kyo's warmth. It reminded me of how Usato used to do pretty much the same thing.

"I wonder what Usato is up to?" I said, looking up at the sky while I neatened my hair.

He was my savior, so to speak, and he'd left Luqvist three days ago. I knew that he was headed for Samariarl, but I wondered how far along he was.

"Aw, what's the matter? All lonely and lost now that Usato's gone?"

"No! Not in the slightest," I said, turning away from Kyo's teasing grin.

Kyo was a kind and friendly guy, but he was very fond of goofing around and teasing too.

I don't have any human friends, so just having someone to talk to makes me unbelievably happy . . . Ugh, just thinking about how few friends I had makes me so sad.

"I've been thinking that I'll leave pretty soon," I said.

"Already?"

"Yeah. To be honest—and it might just be me—I don't feel comfortable here anymore."

There was all the attention I was getting, for one thing, but it also felt like people's impression of me had changed. It was like all my classmates and teachers weren't sure how to approach me. At yesterday's practical magic lesson, everyone was so afraid of pairing up with me that it only left *me* feeling hurt. I understood how Usato must have felt about me being so scared of him. Because of all of that, I'd been preparing so that I could leave Luqvist within the week.

"That said, all I really needed to do before leaving was inform my family."

And so, I'd written a letter, the contents of which were inflammatory, as far as my family would be concerned. Kyo, however, already knew I intended to leave, so he followed my gaze to the sky and let out a sigh.

"We sure are going to be lone—" he started before quickly going silent.

"Were you just about to say lonely?"

"Heck no! I'm just going to miss having a convenient way to waste some time, that's all."

I laughed.

"That's the same thing!" I said.

"What?! It's not the same at all!"

Seeing Kyo like that—desperately scrambling for excuses—made me happy. I really felt fulfilled.

"The way you make fun of people, it's just like Usato," said Kyo.

"Seriously?!"

"You're happy?! That wasn't a compliment, you know!"

I guess I'd gotten overly excited because he said we were alike. Kyo let out a frustrated sigh and scratched his head.

"Then again, the way you can flip a downer mood on its head and clear the air . . . you really have been influenced by Usato."

"Well, we're teacher and student, after all."

"Just don't get *too* influenced, okay? However you choose to live your life, you'll never be him. You have to be *you*."

"Don't worry about that," I replied with a shy chuckle. "I don't want to be Usato, I just want to be able to stand alongside him as an equal. That's why I want to leave Luqvist and undertake true rescue team training."

"Hmph. Well, at least you get it," said Kyo.

I suddenly realized that I'd been worrying Kyo without even knowing. I felt a little bad about it as I ate the last of my fruit.

"So, when are you leaving?" he asked.

"If possible, within the week," I replied.

"A bit quick, no?"

"I just figure it's best to strike while the iron is hot. I've made up my mind, so it's time to go. That's why I'm going to visit the headmistress today and tell her that I'm leaving."

Kyo couldn't believe it at first, but he turned to me with a grin.

"Then come over tonight, okay? Me and sis will help you celebrate your new journey."

The moment he spoke the words, I lost all of mine. My heart filled with a feeling I simply couldn't put into words. I'd never, ever had anyone to celebrate my achievements with and Kyo's act of kindness made me happier than I'd ever been.

"I'll be there! I can't wait!" I said.

"That's the spirit. Get your hopes nice and high. Though uh . . . Kiriha is going to be doing all the cooking."

I couldn't help but laugh at Kyo's bashful confession.

"Alright, well, I better be getting home," said Kyo. "So, I guess it's so long for now."

"I guess so."

It was still midday and I'm sure he had things to do. I also had the headmistress to talk to.

"You're heading off to see the headmistress, I assume?" asked Kyo.

"Yep. I mean, it might take a little while . . ."

"Well, we don't mind if you show up late, okay? Good luck, Nack."

Kyo waved goodbye and walked down an alleyway with his fruit. I'd put on a brave front for him, but actually, I was really nervous about meeting with the headmistress. She was the most powerful person in the whole city.

"But I won't get anywhere if I don't take a step forward," I murmured.

That's what the old me did—he just accepted the situation and did nothing about it. But thanks to my five days of training with Usato, I could stand on my own two feet and walk my own path.

"Alright, let's do this," I said, cheering myself on.

I was nervous about meeting the headmistress. I was worried about what she would say, but I would take it all on the chin and keep on moving. If the students at school knew that I was leaving, I bet they wouldn't even believe it. After all, Luqvist was the best place in the entire world for learning magic. And if I'd been really serious about studying and learning my healing magic when I first got here, perhaps I'd never have even considered the idea of leaving.

But it wasn't magic that I wanted to learn anymore.

If I was going to become even half the man that Usato was, then I needed to go to Llinger Kingdom.

"I need to join the rescue team."

* * *

Headmistress Gladys. The most important and powerful person in Luqvist and the person in charge of the Luqvist School of Magic. No doubt she'd be a busy woman—her job meant watching over both the city and its education system and all the responsibilities that came with them. It wouldn't be a simple thing for her to make time for a lone student like myself. I expected that I'd have to wait for a break between duties, and that I might be left in front of her door for quite a while.

"Alright, here we go . . ." I muttered.

I took a deep breath to calm myself, then knocked on the heavy doors of the headmistress's office.

"Nack Agares," came a voice from inside. "Do come in."

I was puzzled. I never imagined that she'd know it was me outside. I timidly opened the door and found Gladys sitting at her desk with a smile. There was another seat in front of her.

"I had a feeling you'd be coming," she said. "Please, take a seat."

"Hm? Oh, erm . . ." I murmured.

How did she know I was coming?

I did as I was told and sat down, but I felt completely out of place in the unique atmosphere of the headmistress's office. I could barely even bring myself to move.

What is going on? This doesn't have something to do with Usato, does it? I don't have any proof, but I can't help thinking this is his doing . . . and I think I'm right.

"Um, do you perhaps know . . . *why* I'm here?" I asked.

"You're here because you intend to leave the school, yes?"

Gladys's expression never changed, but I felt my brow furrow internally.

Now that I've come, will she try and keep me here?

I had expected that it wasn't going to be easy. Even if it was in name only, I was still technically a noble enrolled at the school. I just hadn't expected things to play out in this way.

I may have made a huge mistake . . .

The headmistress tilted her head, confused by the look of torment and suffering on my face.

"Hm? Oh, Nack, I think you may have the wrong idea," she said.

"Wait, what? Aren't you going to try and stop me from leaving . . . ?"

Gladys let a wry chuckle escape her lips. I realized then that I really *did* have the wrong idea.

"Let's try not to jump to conclusions, yes?"

"Oh, um, okay."

"Please don't worry. Now, while it *is* sad to see one such as yourself decide to leave our school, I respect your decision."

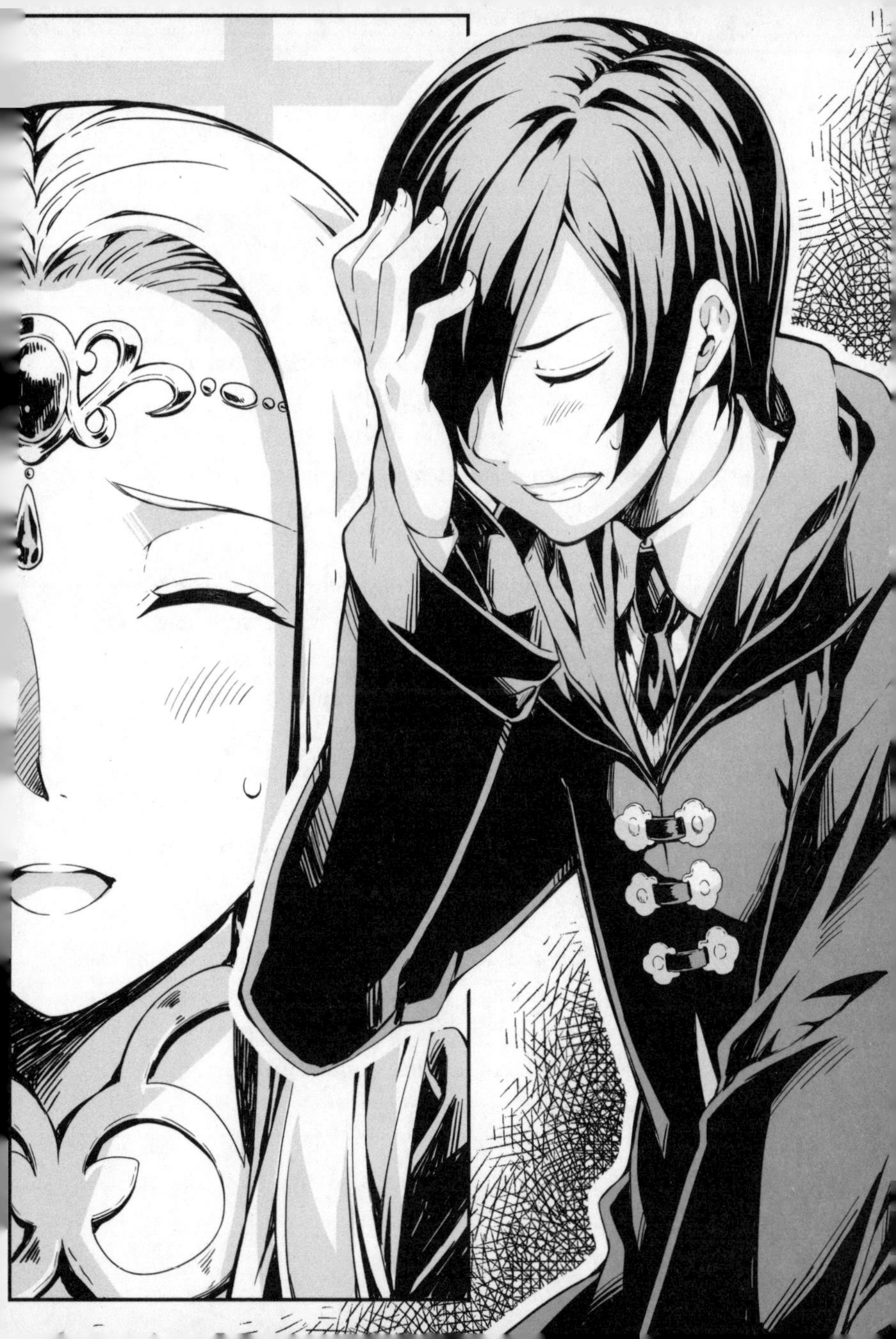

So wait, she's not trying to stop me . . . she's doing the opposite?

"So, you're not going to interrogate me about all the training that Usato put me through and then try and put other people through the same thing?" I asked.

Gladys had been resting her elbows on her desk, but the moment I asked my question, she collapsed on top of it. She quickly regained her composure and forced a quivering smile onto her face.

"I-I would never dream of doing such a thing," she replied. "Making an ordinary child undergo such treatment would break them entirely in just a matter of days. Such training is for healers and healers only—it's entirely impractical otherwise."

It was a harsh appraisal, but it was also true. Usato had claimed that he was going easy on me, but even just my first day of training was, in a word, insane. I felt the fear in those old memories rushing back. I shook my head to clear them from my mind.

"But how did you know I was coming?" I asked.

That was, first and foremost, what I was most curious about. It was just too weird that the headmistress knew what I was up to.

"Well, you underwent Usato's unique instruction in the ways of healing magic," she replied gently.

"Yes."

"His training methods . . . that is to say, the rescue team's training methods, are unlike anything here at our school of magic. The training was all encompassing—you strengthened your magic, your body, and your mind. And now that you have experienced such a thing, you feel that something is missing in the lessons here at Luqvist, do you not?"

The headmistress had hit the nail right on the head. Ever since my battle with Mina, every lesson I'd taken felt lacking. And when it came to basic sparring, the sheer speed I'd developed in my legs let me take the initiative and win with ease. I'd never been very good at lessons in hand-to-hand combat, but now I could read my opponent's movements with ease.

"I had always intended to leave eventually," I said, "but in this short time I've realized that I can't get any stronger through lessons at the school."

I didn't want to sound rude or ungrateful, but now that I'd been through the hell of Usato's training, everything I went through at school just felt too easy and too gentle.

"Sudden change isn't always entirely good. There are downsides to it as well. In your case, your whole sense of value shifted. I could see this, and so I waited for you to come."

"I . . . I see."

She was worried about me . . .

I looked down at the floor. All this time, I'd been avoiding the truth of the matter. I knew that I'd gotten stronger because of my training, but I'd never thought my physical abilities now put me leagues above the rest of my classmates. It made me happy to think that I was a little closer to reaching Usato's heights, but the difference between my abilities and my perception of them left me confused.

"Nack," said Gladys. "You have gotten very strong."

She spoke kindly to me as I stared at the ground. There was a mix of confusion and happiness swirling within me.

"I watched your training with Usato," she continued. "I don't mean to sound rude, but on many occasions I questioned his sanity. On the times that he . . . got serious, so to speak, many of our teachers believed that he was a monster finally showing its true colors."

"Yeah, that makes perfect sense," I said, lifting my head and nodding at the headmistress.

When Usato changed like that, he was so utterly terrifying that I was convinced he was a different person.

"However, you persevered, you overcame his training, and it brought you victory in your match against Mina Lycia. You should be proud of yourself. You and your victory are now etched into the hearts of all who saw it."

"I didn't do anything *that* grand or amazing," I said bashfully.

"It was only a small change, but it was decisive," said the headmistress, placing her hand over her heart. "And everyone here will change because of it."

She closed her eyes for a moment as if feeling something very important, and then she smiled at me.

"I am talking about hard work, effort, and self-belief over talent," she continued. "That is what you and Usato showed the entire Luqvist School of Magic. It was something that we teachers were unable to do on our own."

I had a feeling that Usato didn't care about that in the slightest when he trained me. I was so desperate just to keep up that I didn't even have time to think about the bigger picture, either. And yet, I was proud of myself. It made me really happy to think that the work Usato and I did left a positive influence.

"And so, I wanted to let you know that I am grateful. Thank you, Nack."

"You're welcome!" I said brightly.

The headmistress nodded sagely, then her expression darkened slightly.

"Unlike the two of you, we teachers . . . were powerless. We thought only of maintaining the state of the school. Because of that, we were unable to help you when you needed us."

"It's not the school's fault that I was bullied," I replied.

"No, it is a truth that cannot be overlooked," said Gladys sadly, "and I feel nothing but apologetic to you for it."

She really does care about all of us students.

I knew that the problem between Mina and me wasn't one that the school could easily insert itself into. But even then, the headmistress still looked extremely regretful for being unable to rescue me.

"Until a little while ago, I tried to pretend like the last two years of bullying just never happened," I said.

I wanted to settle things between Mina and me so I could move on and never see her ever again. That was what had driven me to win in our fight.

"What she did to me was really, truly awful," I said, "and it's deeper than just a matter of forgiveness."

I'd lived my life thinking that none of it was me—that all of it was the people around me.

"But she cried," I admitted.

"Oh?"

When Mina had tried to use her imperfect mana boost, I'd grabbed her hands to try and keep her magic power under control. That was the first time I'd ever seen her cry in front of anyone.

"I knew her when we were both little, so I know she's not the type to cry because she's hurt. She won't easily cry in front of other people, either."

In fact, until that moment, I'd never seen Mina cry before. That was how strong she was.

"All I ever thought about was myself," I said. "I felt like my unfair circumstances were everybody else's fault. But when I saw Mina cry, I felt like I'd been wrong about it all."

"What do you mean?"

"I think Mina and I both got things wrong. She'd never admit it in a million years, but I think if I'd been more aware of the people around me when I first got here, then perhaps we could have been friends, just like when we were kids."

If that had happened, I never would have encountered Usato the way that I did. But in any case, there was no use lingering on what could have been.

"Headmistress Gladys," I said. "I'm going to stay positive. Mina bullied me, that's true, but now things are different. I'm going to live a life where I don't have to avoid her. I'm going to live a life where I can look her in the eyes."

Yes, I was scared, but at the same time, that was only a small part of my heart. Until now, I'd been walking dark paths with nowhere to go, but now the road ahead was clear with a goal at the end of it. Gladys was at first surprised by my confident gaze, but she soon relaxed into a smile.

"You really have gotten stronger," she remarked. "Far stronger than I'd imagined."

She closed her eyes, which quivered with happiness. A silence fell over the room, and I waited for what she would say next.

"Nack," she said finally. "You're leaving here because you want to join the rescue team, yes?"

"That's right," I said, sitting up straight.

"Then I will prepare your travel to the Llinger Kingdom."

"What?!"

I'd never even asked for that kind of treatment.

What is going on?!

"I'm really happy for the offer," I said, "but are you sure?"

"It'll take you a whole week on foot, no? Let me help you get there safely."

My idea was to ask a traveling merchant if I could tag along with them on the way to Llinger Kingdom, but there certainly wasn't any harm in taking a more secure route.

"But is it really okay to give such special treatment to a student?" I asked.

"I don't expect that to be an issue," replied the headmistress. "Once I approve of your request to leave the school, our relationship will no longer be that of headmistress and student. We'll simply be friends, so there's no problem."

I felt like she was really straining the logic of what she was saying, but I could at least follow her basic reasoning. It was impressive stuff.

"You'll have to deal with Rose when you join the rescue team, so give it your best," said Gladys brightly.

"You mean Usato's teacher?"

"Yes. She's the captain of the rescue team. She taught Usato when he started out. She's the strongest healer we've ever known."

"The strongest healer ever . . ."

"Perhaps a slight overstatement, but it *is* true to say that nobody has ever surpassed her physical abilities. I've never seen anyone who beats her as a healer . . . well, not yet."

When I thought of how crazy Usato was, it made all the sense in the world that his teacher was just as ridiculously strong. But the headmistress must have seen all kinds of magic in her lifetime, so if *she* could say that about Rose, then just how powerful was Rose?

"I heard from Usato that she carried the aura of a wild carnivorous beast," I said.

"And he's not wrong. There's always a terrifying aura surrounding her."

Gladys cringed for a moment as if thinking back to the past, but then she turned a serious gaze onto me.

"I'm sure you're already well aware, but the rescue team training is no ordinary training," she said. "And to be perfectly honest, until Usato came along, the idea of her even having a disciple was frankly unbelievable."

"How so?"

"Rose's standard for healers is ridiculously high. You see, what she's looking for is . . ." Gladys paused for a moment before going on. "She's trying to create a healer just like herself."

"What?"

My thoughts seemed to freeze in my mind.

"You trained under Usato, so you've never actually experienced Rose's real training. Usato, on the other hand, came here with her stamp of approval. Her training is beyond extreme, and he got through it."

"Wow, Usato is really incredible, isn't he?"

"He might not see it himself, but he's Rose's ideal rescue team member. Given his performance in the battle against the Demon Lord's forces, he's as strong as they come. He's performing not just up to her expectations, he's exceeding them."

I had very little idea what sort of a person Rose was. I had an image of her as a total monster, one who could lift mountains—a person who had made Usato into a violent and powerful beast of his own. Now, thanks to the headmistress's words, I was starting to believe she was even *worse* than that.

"There's really no need to worry, Nack," said Headmistress Gladys, "Rose's intense strictness stands out the most, but she also hides a kinder, gentler side. That Usato respects her and follows her as one of her subjects is proof of that."

"Oh, uh . . . is that . . . so?"

I couldn't help thinking it unwise to put my faith in an invisible kindness. Gladys took little notice of my awkward expression as she went on.

"Rose treats everybody the same, no matter who they are."

"Should I assume that means she's equally strict on everyone?"

Gladys went silent.

Oh come on, this is where you're supposed to reassure me, no? Now I'm just going to head into this next part of my journey worried sick.

"Nack," said the headmistress, "Rose is so much more than you can even imagine. And in meeting her, you may face hardships . . . actually, no. You *will* face hardships. There's no doubting that."

"So you're guaranteeing it? There's no way around them?"

"I'd give up on trying to escape the suffering. Rose is the very definition of unreasonable."

My image of Rose suddenly grew into something far worse than when I first came here. But at the same time, I wouldn't really know anything until I actually met her for myself. That was just as true for Rose as it was for the rescue team that served under her command—all her scary-looking rescue team members and the demon girl they called the Black Knight. Then there were the two healers outside of the rescue team whom Usato had told me about.

"But even then, I'll meet others through the experience, won't I? And for me, the connections I make may well be unforgettable."

Gladys giggled.

"Oh yes, I guarantee that wholeheartedly."

"In which case, I'm going."

There was no reason for me to stop here. No matter how

much suffering I had to go through for the rescue team training, I was not about to abandon my goal. The headmistress smiled at the determination she saw in me and nodded.

"Which means there's nothing more to be said. Tell me, when are you thinking of leaving?"

"Preferably within the week, but . . . is that possible?"

"You young people are so quick to spring into action, aren't you? I'll do my very best to set you up with transport by the end of the week."

"Thank you so much!"

I leaped from my chair and bowed deeply to the headmistress. I knew that I was asking a lot from her, but I was overjoyed to know that I'd be able to leave so soon. I glanced out the window and realized that we'd been talking for quite a while—the sun was already setting. I figured now that my school departure was settled, I should take my leave of the headmistress—by the time I got to Kiriha and Kyo's house, dinner would probably be ready.

"Well then, I'd best be going," I said. "Thank you so much for everything."

"Think nothing of it. I learned a lot from both you and Usato. Do your very best, Nack. I look forward to seeing how far you go."

I laughed.

"I bet it's not going to be easy getting there," I said.

I bowed again. The headmistress waved goodbye as I left her office. Us students didn't get many—if any—opportunities to talk to the headmistress one to one, but I learned through our conversation that she really did have her students' best interests at heart.

"I can't believe she knew I was leaving before I said anything," I said, chuckling to myself. "I must have looked like a fool."

I walked the school's corridors as the sun continued to set. Lots of students were heading home now that all the classes for the day were over.

"This might be the last time I ever see this place," I muttered to myself.

I didn't have a single fond memory of the Luqvist School of Magic—it was all just me getting bullied by Mina and me being down and out about my healing magic. Still, for everything that had happened, I had nonetheless spent two years of my life here. For me, this was now a starting point—it was where my life truly began. And when I thought of it that way, I felt a little reluctant to leave, even though the place had meant so little to me.

Just then, a girl who was about to walk by me spotted something behind me and shrieked before running away.

"Hm?" I murmured.

Was that because of me?

I couldn't help but feel a little surprised by the girl's reaction. I then realized that she'd been looking behind me. I breathed a sigh of relief and turned around only to find myself once again surprised.

"Wha?!"

All the students that had been walking behind me were pressed up against the walls, their faces pale as they panicked to clear the corridor for a single student to walk by unimpeded. He had gray hair and a brimming smile, and when he noticed me, he casually waved.

"Why hello there, Nack," he said.

"H-Halpha . . . ?" I stammered.

* * *

Halpha.

If you asked anyone at school who they were most afraid of, this was the name they'd utter. Halpha was aggressive, cutthroat, and cold blooded, but he went about his violence with a smile plastered to his face. His magical eye abilities could shut down almost any mage. Almost everyone who faced him left with their spirits crushed.

And now, for reasons I could not fully comprehend, I was walking side by side with him. We'd met on a few occasions, but I'd almost never talked to him face to face before.

"I can't tell you how long it's been since I've had company for the trip home," said Halpha.

So why are we walking home together?

Halpha turned to me with a smile as I grappled with my inner turmoil.

"Something wrong?" he asked.

"Er, no . . . but, um, sorry. Your smile is terrifying."

It wasn't as scary as Usato's was, but it was still a unique kind of frightening. Halpha looked taken aback for a moment but quickly relaxed into an easier smile.

"That means I failed," he said. "Hm. So that smile was no good, huh? And I've been trying so hard to put people at ease with it. It's so unfortunate that it hasn't been working."

"*That* was your attempt at a smile?!" I said, mystified.

But your eyes were ice cold the whole time! If anything, you looked like you were scheming something! I'll give you full marks for trying to look shady!

Halpha chuckled. He seemed to enjoy my reaction. This confused me greatly.

"You aren't scared of me," stated Halpha plainly.

I gasped.

Until recently, I'd been so petrified of Halpha that I avoided being anywhere near him at all times. But now things were different—even though I was scared of him, I could talk to him like I would anyone else.

"I suppose it's because I met someone even scarier," I replied.

"You mean Usato?"

"Yeah. Compared to him, you're fine."

When Usato was in training mode, his expression and the way he spoke to me was so scary that it scraped away at my very soul. Now that I'd spent three days with that side of him, everything else was totally bearable.

"But I have to ask," I said. "Why are you walking with me, Halpha?"

Halpha put a finger to his jaw for a few moments before answering.

"I just feel like it," he stated.

This was not the answer I was expecting. Astonishment was written all over me.

"But if you pushed me for more of an answer," he continued, "it's because I wanted the chance to talk to you."

"Me? But outside of Usato, there's nothing interesting about me at all."

"But this is enjoyable for me," said Halpha. "It's been so long since I could just talk to someone without them being petrified or otherwise feeling something spiteful or hateful toward me."

"Oh, I uh, I see."

I felt like Halpha's words gave me a tiny glimpse into his

life. It was no wonder people were scared of him—in battle he was utterly merciless with more than enough power to back it up. And yet, that also meant that life at school for him was, in some ways, very lonely.

Huh?! What is this feeling?!

Halpha was the strongest person in the entire school, while I was just a healer who, until very recently, had spent his entire life here getting bullied. And yet, all the same, here I was feeling something like a kinship between us, but our positions couldn't have been farther apart.

"Erm, I still have some time," I said, "so why don't we talk for a bit?"

Halpha's eyes went wide with curiosity, but when they met with my own, he burst into a grin.

"I would like that very much," he replied.

And so, Halpha and I ventured into a somewhat awkward attempt at everyday conversation. The more we talked, the more I realized that Halpha was more human than people gave him credit for. Sure, he was a little overly aggressive and his smile was terrifying. His words always felt like they hid a deeper and more mysterious meaning, but inside he hurt just like the rest of us.

"I see," said Halpha. "So you're leaving rather soon then?"

"That's right," I replied.

I'd just finished telling him about my plans to join the rescue team. Halpha nodded, impressed.

"I must say," he said, "it's so *very* exciting to think that someday you might be just as powerful as Usato."

Whoa! He's got super-high expectations!

While it always hurt to have people say negative things about you, now I was realizing that when truly strong people like Halpha put their hopes in you, that too came with its own extremely heavy weight.

"Do you hope to one day work as a member of the rescue team?" asked Halpha.

"Yes. But, of course, I have to prove I'm good enough to join them first."

"While I'd love to tell you you're already strong enough, all I have to go on is Usato's example. If he's the baseline, becoming a full-fledged member may be quite the challenge."

"Yeah, I guess I really won't know until I'm there."

Usato himself had said I'd have no trouble getting in. He'd said that to cheer me up, but if I really didn't make it into the team, I'd feel awful. The thought of it made my shoulders slump. I let out a dejected sigh. Halpha saw the look on my face, and he looked worried as he covered his eyes with his hands.

"Oh my, I made you worry, didn't I?" he said. "It's times like this that I so hate the way I comment on things so heartlessly."

"It's fine. It's the truth. And, also, I'm not *too* worried about it."

Halpha hadn't said anything wrong. I really didn't know yet if I had what it took to join the rescue team. Even with Usato's seal of approval, if I messed up at some point, that would mean no rescue team for me.

Usato had helped me to better learn healing magic, and through his training I'd improved my physical abilities. From here on out, the rest was up to me. And I would make sure, come hell or high water, that I would live up to Usato's expectations.

Without thinking, my right hand scrunched up into a fist—a manifestation of my will.

Halpha chuckled at the sight.

"It looks like I underestimated you, Nack," he said.

"Really?"

"Yes. I can see it in you. You're many times stronger than you once were."

I felt suddenly bashful to hear such a compliment from one so strong. I scratched the back of my head while Halpha took a step forward out in front of me.

"You've spent all this time talking to me about yourself, but a one-sided conversation isn't particularly fair, is it? Allow me to talk about myself a little."

"You're going to tell me about yourself?"

"Indeed."

Halpha's purple eyes lit up as he turned to face me. It was

his magical sight, a magic within the rare field of magical eyes. It allowed him to see one's powers and the flow of their magical energy. It frightened me a little to be on the other end of it, but all the same, I stood tall and held Halpha's gaze.

"I've been able to see the flow of magic in people since I was quite young," said Halpha.

"So, from when you were about seven or eight?"

That was about the time at which people awakened to their magical abilities. However, in answer to my question, Halpha shook his head.

"No, I was far younger than that. I've had this magic since as far back as I can remember. Back then, I was enamored by the idea of fighting with magic. Launching fireballs and lightning bolts from your hands, crafting ice—that was what I looked up to. However, I was left cursing fate for the magical eyes it gave me."

I understood his feelings. I understood them so well that it hurt. Your magic type was something you were born with—it was a reality that you simply had to accept because it was impossible to change, no matter how much you struggled. Just like Halpha with his magical eyes, I too had once hated my healing magic.

"So what happened next?" I asked.

"Well, I knew that getting mad about it was pointless, so I just accepted the situation."

"That's pretty straightforward."

"I've never been one to get hung up on things," said Halpha plainly. "Once I accepted that I was stuck with my eyes, all I could think about was how I could use them to fight. That was pretty much my childhood in a nutshell."

"That's a uh . . . terrifying thought," I said.

I didn't have any other words—Halpha must have been incredibly strong willed as a child. But I felt like I understood now why he had developed into the person he had.

"And then you came to Luqvist?" I asked.

"Yes. There's so much magic here of all different kinds. I thought the place would give me some insights," Halpha said, looking down at his hands. "However, in the end, I couldn't find what I was looking for here."

There was something about his words—they echoed with a certain futility.

"The people here didn't agree with my opinions. They attempted to convince me otherwise. They said things like, 'magical eyes can't be used in battle', and told me to find more helpful ways to put my magic to use."

"But you couldn't let go of what you believed, could you?"

"Nope. They talked and they reasoned and they admonished me, but it didn't matter—I wasn't the kind of meek and obedient kid who would just follow their orders."

He spoke the words with a smile, but there was such

animosity in Halpha's comment that I couldn't help flinching in response. I got the strong impression that Halpha was the sort of person who spoke his mind openly and that he'd been like that for a long time.

"So I stopped asking the people around me for their opinions," continued Halpha. "As such, this school is no longer a place where I undertake instruction but rather a place I can use to strengthen my own skills."

"Uh-huh . . ."

I could see how things had grown from there. Now the reason that Halpha was so feared among the students was crystal clear.

"Where there's a will, there's a way," said Halpha. "In my case, all I could see was the flow of magical energy, so I taught myself how to use that for battle. As a result, I developed my own unique fighting style—one in which I lock my opponents down by perfectly reading their movements."

That's just not normal, if you ask me . . .

I wasn't going to say that to Halpha's face, but who could have even imagined that? Who could have thought that he'd develop his magical eyes into a murderous technique that was perfect against magic users? I had a feeling that Halpha put his classmates at the time through something not unlike a unique hell.

"And, well, that brought me here," said Halpha, "but to be honest, I'm getting bored."

"Oh? Why's that?"

"Nobody will fight me. How am I supposed to develop my skills if I don't have partners to work with?"

Anybody who fought Halpha could be completely healed with healing magic, but that didn't mean you could easily wipe away the fear of having your weak points targeted and the pain that came when they were hit. I had to imagine it would traumatize most people so bad that they'd never want to stand in front of Halpha again.

"That's why, though it was not my intent, I thoroughly enjoyed my sparring contest with Usato."

"You enjoyed that?"

"Well, I lost, but yes."

I couldn't believe he could say that, but then again, that was Usato for you. He had his ways. Halpha chuckled as he went on.

"I don't like to lose, but I felt my limits when Usato defeated me, and it filled me with a desire to grow even stronger."

"Er, Halpha?" I asked, suddenly scared.

Halpha ignored me.

"I'm going to have to further develop my powers of observation to ensure I'm not caught by similar feints ever again. However, it might be better to strengthen my body first. Now that I can see how much more there is to do, I realize that I was conceited. If you're too proud of what you are, you'll lack the true subconscious will to grow more powerful. The next time I meet Usato, I'm going to ask him for another round so that I can find whatever new weak points have emerged."

Halpha's face was a terrifying thing to look at. And not only that, his aura was so overwhelming that I took two steps away from him without even realizing it. Even the people around us in town had stopped and were looking at him in wonder. Some of them even looked on the verge of fainting. Fighting against my own instincts, and knowing it was a little rude, I gave Halpha a pat on the shoulder.

"Halpha," I said, "you might want to cool down a touch, yeah?"

"Oh, I apologize," Halpha replied, scratching his cheek bashfully. "It seems I lost myself in thought for a moment."

Suddenly, all the people around us were looking at *me* in confusion—they couldn't believe that I could so casually calm a monster with a light pat on the shoulder. But it wasn't just them—I couldn't believe that I did it, either.

And then I realized that Halpha was standing with his arms crossed, staring at me in silence.

"Um, what's wrong? Why are you staring at me like that?" I asked.

"It just occurred to me as I was thinking about my own strength . . . when I look at you and Usato, well . . ."

"Well?"

"I can't help but think that it might not be a bad idea if *I* were to go to the Llinger Kingdom, too."

"What?!"

"Oh, don't get me wrong. I don't mean right away. I was just thinking of it as a potential option later down the line. I still haven't graduated, you know."

For a moment, I thought he was saying he would go with me to Llinger.

But still, his words jolted me.

"But what would you do at Llinger Kingdom, Halpha?"

"I could become a knight. Before Usato visited, I was thinking of becoming one of Samariarl's knights. But now that I've made Usato's acquaintance, the idea of joining the Llinger Kingdom's forces is also appealing."

"Wow," I said.

"That, and Luqvist is much closer."

Halpha's last addition seemed to erase all the weight in his earlier statement.

"There's also one more reason," said Halpha.

"It's not because the food is delicious or something like that, is it?" I asked exasperated.

Halpha chuckled.

"Oh, perhaps that's a good reason also . . . but no. Simply put, it strikes me as the kind of nation that would embrace a magical-eye user like myself."

"Oh, I see," I said.

"Ordinarily speaking, the idea of a magical-eye user becoming a knight is preposterous. Such people might be turned away before they even get the chance to take the entry exam. But I've since heard that Llinger judges people not by their magical type but by their actual ability, and that, to me, gives it great value."

Superiority was something often determined by one's magic. That was especially true with knights, who spent much of their time in battle. But the Llinger Kingdom was a place without such discrimination. That made it a potential bright future for Halpha.

"I have to say though," I ventured, "I can't see you as a knight."

"I'm well aware of that—even I can't imagine myself decked out in armor and swinging a sword around."

Halpha used his speed and agility to read his opponents and intercept their movements. If he had to wear armor, his speed would be hampered.

"Then again, I feel like you could cut down your foes by reading their movements and landing fierce counter shots. It's like, if you can't take victory with your first blow, you can at least severely punish your enemy for theirs," I chuckled at the thought. "But it's not like you at all to give your opponent any initiative, is it?"

"You might be onto something," remarked Halpha.

"Hm?"

"Ah, yes. I see, I see," said Halpha, thinking. "Fatal counter shots. What a most wonderful thing you've just brought to my attention. Instead of intercepting my opponent's first move, I could *give* them a perceived opening just to land an even *more* powerful counter strike. I don't think I'm capable of such a thing at present, but if I train those skills . . ."

Oh no! Halpha's making that terrifying face again! His pursuit of strength is inhuman!

"Halpha! Halpha! Come back to me!" I cried.

"Huh . . .? Oh. Did I lose myself in my thoughts again?"

"Just how often do you do that?" I asked, exasperated.

Still, I was impressed by his drive to improve and grow. He was completely different than me. When I learned I was a healer, I gave up completely. Halpha, on the other hand, ignored all the criticism thrown his way, and in his pursuit of strength, he'd carved out a place for himself. To top things off, he still wasn't done—he was aiming to become even *more* powerful.

And just like that, I realized that I respected him.

"You're amazing, Halpha," I remarked.

Halpha responded with a bashful grin. Although he seemed for a moment skeptical of my compliment, he relaxed into a smile a moment afterward.

"I think *you're* the amazing one, Nack," he replied.

"But I was just a complete nobody until recently," I said. "I was helpless, lost, and stuck at the whims of whoever wanted to push me around."

"But that's exactly what is so amazing. Under Usato's tutelage, you crawled up and over the adversity that faced you, and you overcame it. It is not easy for people to confront their tormentors face to face, but you accepted your own fears, and it earned you a victory over Mina Lycia."

Halpha put a hand on my shoulder, then went on.

"You are a nobody no more, and you are far from helpless now. There is no need for you to put yourself down any longer. In your victory over Mina, you became one of the strong."

"Halpha," I uttered.

"You are a person who knows hard work and the power of effort. I hold those who know such things in very high regard. I will never respect those who blame their losses on the 'talents' of their opponents. You worked hard, and you earned what you got. And that, simply put, is amazing."

It reminded me of something that Kyo had said to me.

Halpha is merciless. He judges people only on whether they are strong or weak.

But, actually, that wasn't true. Halpha watched people closely. He didn't think about people in terms of strong or weak, but rather whether or not they were working to reach what they wanted. It was clear to me now that Halpha hated those who gave up on improving themselves and stopped believing in their own potential. He hated people who simply decided things were impossible and refused to stand up for themselves ... just like the sort of person I once was.

Halpha only opened his heart to those he felt were seriously giving life their best efforts.

"Be confident in yourself, Nack," he said.

"I will," I said, though I could hear my own voice wavering.

Halpha was an easy person to misunderstand, but I felt like now I had an understanding of who he was. He was the strongest person in the Luqvist School of Magic, but also the loneliest person, too. Halpha took his hand off my shoulder and turned. He started to walk back the way we had come.

"Well then, I should be heading home," he said.

"Um, thank you, Halpha," I said.

"No, no, thank *you*. It's been a long time since I had such a fun discussion with someone."

I'd been so scared of him to begin with, but now, talking to Halpha felt entirely natural.

If only I'd talked to him sooner ... but then again, it's only because I am who I am now that I **could** *talk to him. As the old me, I would have turned tail and fled the moment I saw his face.*

"I'm sad to hear that you'll be leaving so soon," said Halpha, "but more than that, I'm looking forward to seeing where your efforts take you."

I laughed.

"That's exactly what the headmistress said to me."

"That just means we see the same things in you. And I bet it's not just us—Kiriha, Kyo, and Usato all expect great things from you."

Wow, talk about responsibilities.

And yet, they weren't such a bad thing to shoulder. I had to chuckle at how I once hated the idea of expectations in all forms. How much I'd changed.

"We'll meet again," I said, "and when we do, I'll be strong enough to fight you!"

"Nothing would make me happier," said Halpha with a laugh. "That just means I'm going to have to work especially hard to make sure I don't lose."

I could see by the smile on his face that I'd set his competitive spirit alight. I'd brought that on myself, sure, but it was also just another reason for me to work hard and grow stronger. Halpha waved and I watched him walk back toward the school. Then I gave myself a slap on the cheeks with both hands to get myself together and started walking again.

"Wow, it's gotten pretty dark," I muttered.

The last light of sunset was fading, and the night sky was stretching out above my head. The magical lanterns around the city began to light up, illuminating the way for its citizens.

"Perfect timing for dinner, perhaps."

Kyo and Kiriha were waiting. The thought made me happy. I felt a lightness in my step. So much had happened in just one day, but it still wasn't over yet.

* * *

By the time I made it to Kiriha and Kyo's house, the sun had completely set. There wasn't much in the way of lighting in their neighborhood, so it was often completely dark. But it was easier to navigate the paths today thanks to the bright light of the moon. I arrived at their house and gave the front door a light knock.

"Coming!" said Kiriha, who opened up the door to greet me. "You're just in time, Nack. Dinner is almost ready. Come in and sit down."

"Thank you so much for having me today," I said, taking a seat at the table.

"Come on now, no need to be so uptight."

A moment later, Kyo walked into the room, yawning.

"Oh, Nack," he said. "You came."

"Yes, but it took a bit longer than I thought," I replied.

"Looks like your talk with the headmistress went well."

I nodded.

"Yes. We talked about a lot of things, but she's okay with me leaving the school."

"Glad to hear it."

Kyo took a seat in front of me and rested his head on his hands. I could tell by his smile that he really was glad. We chatted for a bit, and then Kiriha brought dinner out. It was much more luxurious than anything I'd been served when I was living with them before.

How much did they spend on this?

I turned to Kiriha with a worried look. She smiled.

"Don't worry about it," she said. "We spent a little extra but nothing that will break the bank."

"To be completely honest," added Kyo, "we used the money Usato gave us, so we didn't even-hurk?!"

Kiriha punched the chuckling Kyo as she put the food on the table.

"Not another word out of you," she said, sighing. "Sometimes I wonder if my little brother will ever grow up . . ."

"We're twins!" he said. "We're the same age!"

"I'm not talking about age. I'm talking about behavior, you twit."

When all the food was on the table, Kiriha let out another sigh and took a seat next to Kyo. There was so much more variety than usual—soup, bread, meat, and salad—and it all looked delectable.

"Um, are you sure about all of this?" I asked. "You won't be left starving after I leave because you splurged on this, right?"

"Don't worry about it," said Kiriha.

"What she said," added Kyo. "And anyway, you think Kiriha's the type of weakling to collapse because she doesn't have enough to eat? Get out of town!"

Kyo cackled with laughter as his sister shot him a death glare. It was true, though—Kiriha didn't look at all weak. In fact, she gave Kyo a very strong elbow in the ribs as I turned my attention back to the table.

"Looks great," I said as I took a sip from the soup.

Delicious as always.

"N-Nack . . . aren't you a little too calm and collected? I'm suffering here . . ."

I had elected to indulge in the food while Kyo groaned in pain.

"Well, you only got what you asked for," I said. "Speaking to Kiriha that way was always going to land you in hot water."

"Yeah, you tell him, Nack," added Kiriha.

Kyo shifted in his seat, recomposed himself, then began eating like nothing had happened. We were all just used to conversations playing out this way.

"I heard from Kyo that you're leaving for Llinger soon?" said Kiriha.

"Yes. The headmistress said she'd organize transport for me, so I'll head out as soon as preparations are complete."

"The headmistress is going to do that for you? But why?"

"Um, she said she wanted to thank me."

It was a little complicated, but I gave them a quick rundown. Kiriha nodded, impressed.

"Well, it does feel a bit quick, but if you've made up your mind, then we're behind you. Just make sure you don't leave with any regrets, okay?"

"No problem," I said. "This is the path that I chose for myself, after all."

"Well, if you can say that openly and honestly, I think you'll be fine," said Kiriha with a smile. "And it means we can see you off without any worries."

"You're like an old woman," murmured Kyo, only to once again receive a hard elbow to the ribs. His moans filled the room as Kiriha dug her elbow in and looked at me.

"By the way, what are you going to do about your luggage?" she asked. "Are you going to box it all up and send it?"

"Oh, right. My things," I muttered.

I hadn't even thought about it.

"Well, I'm only taking the bare essentials," I said. "All I have at my house at the moment is a change of clothes and my class textbooks.

"Ah, I see . . . Wait. House? Did you say house just now?"

Kiriha's eyes went wide.

"My parents abandoned me completely, but they were still worried about their reputation," I explained. "They didn't want me living in the dorms because they didn't want people getting the wrong idea. So, my dad ended up getting me a massive house."

"All in the name of appearances?"

"Yep."

For the nobility, keeping up appearances was paramount. If my parents sent me to Luqvist to learn magic and I didn't live in a manner befitting of the nobility, rumors would start to circulate about my family's wealth. So my dad, conceited as he was, spent an exorbitant amount of money to get me a house.

"But after he got me the house, he didn't do anything else at all," I said. "I do all the washing, cooking, and cleaning myself. I would have been better off living in the dorms."

My father provided me only surface-level support. When I thought about it now, he really was completely ridiculous. Who buys a teenager a house?

"It's been rough for you, huh?" said Kiriha.

"I guess even nobles don't always have it easy," added Kyo. "Not that I thought much of them to begin with."

"It really is a struggle," I admitted. "There's no future to speak of, learning all the etiquette is a major pain, and you always have to put up a strong front for appearances. I wouldn't think much of it either."

"Oh, uh . . . are you okay, Nack?" asked Kiriha.

I'd gotten a little too lost in my thoughts and worried her

and Kyo. All of a sudden, I found myself thinking about my little sister. She had so much more potential than I did. She was so kind. I wanted to see her again, but I pushed the feelings away and sipped at my cup of tea.

"I was disowned by my family, so the rest of my life is completely up to me. I can live it however I want. To be honest, it's refreshing—I finally feel free."

Now that I'd sent my last letter to my family, I was no longer a member of the nobility. I'm sure that made things more convenient for them, but if for some reason they tried to take me back, I was ready to run away.

"Kyo, you could learn from Nack," said Kiriha. "He lived all on his own. It's about time you picked up a few more chores."

"Why would you suddenly choose now to start pointing fingers at me? Are you not following the flow of the conversation or what?!"

"Sooner or later you're going to have to start waking up on your own," said Kiriha. "Usato wakes up even earlier than I do."

"Which just means he wakes up way too early!"

Usato woke up just before sunrise. He said that mornings were when he did his daily training.

Maybe I'll try and do morning training too. But anyway, I should probably change the subject, for Kyo's sake . . .

"Oh yeah, I forgot to mention it earlier, but I met Halpha before I came here," I said.

I wanted to tell Kiriha and Kyo about the new side of him I'd discovered. I hoped maybe it might be a chance for them to get along, or . . . at the very least, to talk normally with one another. After I told them what Halpha and I had talked about, Kiriha rested her head on her hands.

"Halpha, huh . . ." she muttered.

"He's a bit of a weird one when it comes to his pursuit of strength, sure, but he's a good guy at heart. That's why I thought maybe you two could try talking to him, get to know him, you know?"

"You just called him a weird one," said Kyo. "You really know how to subtly put people down, Nack. I mean, he *is* a weird one, but still."

I only said that because of that look I saw on his face whenever he got lost in thoughts of his own training. But putting that aside, I felt pretty relaxed around him. I'd gone into our conversation assuming he was little more than a person with a very dangerous fighting style and a personality to match, but I couldn't have been more wrong.

"I just . . . I'm not good at dealing with that smile of his," muttered Kyo, scratching his head.

"Apparently, that's him doing his best to look friendly to the people around him," I said.

"Are you for real? His own efforts are totally stabbing him in the back, then. He's *really* trying to be friendly with people?"

"Yeah."

"What the heck?" uttered Kyo. "Now I don't even know what to do the next time I see him."

Halpha was aloof and awkward. But all people had sides to them that were surprising or unexpected. I'd learned that from talking with Mina.

"Alright, Nack," said Kiriha. "We'll try talking to him like a normal person when we next see him. I mean, we *did* want someone to talk to in class, right Kyo?"

Kyo let out an exaggerated sigh.

"Fine, fine," he said. "I'll try to talk to him as well."

"Kiriha, Kyo . . ." I said, gratefully.

It made me really happy, even though it wasn't me they would be talking to. I was glad that Halpha would have people he could chat with, and that Kiriha and Kyo would have a human outside of me and Usato to chat with too.

"Alright, that's enough talk for now," said Kiriha. "It's time to eat. It wasn't easy to make all of this, so dig in while it's still hot."

"Sounds good!" I said.

It dawned on me then that perhaps this might be the last dinner we shared together. It was in this house that I'd learned warmth and kindness. Before, after I'd collapsed in the streets, when I woke up, I was here in Kiriha and Kyo's house. That had kickstarted my training with Usato. It was all to beat Mina in a battle. Usato had put me through the ringer every session. Afterward, we'd come back here to eat a warm meal. I always felt grateful for Kiriha and Kyo's kindness.

"Everything's happening so fast . . ." I uttered.

The time I spent training with Usato now felt like it was just a tiny sliver of time. And yet, through it, I had discovered so many things that were important to me.

"Hey, Nack," said Kyo. "You're frozen. What's up? If you're not going to eat, I'll totally take your share."

The moment my thoughts drifted, Kyo took my food right out from under my nose.

"No way," I replied. "I'm not going to just give it up. Hey! Why are you taking my plate! That's *my* meat!"

"Like I give a damn! The early bird gets the worm, right?"

"Which means you won't mind if I take *your* food, right Kyo?" said Kiriha.

Kyo quickly handed me my plate back—clearly scared of his sister—and chuckled, though it looked very awkward to me.

"Uh, I'm sorry Nack. I guess I went a little overboard," he said. "Here's your plate."

It hurt to think that I might never see these two fight like this again. I felt a hole open in my heart. Still, I told myself this wouldn't be the last time. I *knew* it wouldn't be the last time. And yet, parting ways still came with a certain sadness. That was why I wanted to make the most of this evening, so I could leave for the Llinger Kingdom feeling bright and positive.

I felt a huge smile growing on my face as I talked and ate with Kiriha and Kyo.

I'm going to burn this memory into my mind so that I never forget it . . .

* * *

The day after my dinner with Kiriha and Kyo, I got a message from the headmistress. It said that in five days' time, a merchant carriage would depart in the morning to take me to Llinger Kingdom.

As soon as I got the message, I started my preparations. But that said, all I had to get ready was my money, a change of clothes, food, and the bare minimum necessary to get by on. Now that I wasn't a student at Luqvist anymore, I went to a shop in town and picked out some clothes and a robe to take with me. I didn't need my uniform, but I'd worn it for the two years I was enrolled at Luqvist. It felt valuable, so I packed it together with my things.

Everything I needed for my trip fit neatly in a rucksack, which surprised even me.

With all my preparations done, all that was left was to wait until the day of departure. When it arrived, I went to Kiriha and

Kyo's place to say goodbye. They'd been especially kind to me, and I wanted to thank them for it.

"I never imagined we'd be seeing you off so soon," said Kiriha. "Good luck out there!"

"Thanks!"

There was a part of me that wanted to stay in Luqvist a little longer. I couldn't help thinking that school would have been more fun together with those two.

"I don't know how rough and tumble the rescue team is, but don't push yourself too hard, yeah?" said Kyo. "Sometimes you have to know when to relax, okay? I feel like you're always kind of tense."

"Says the guy who only knows how to relax . . ." muttered Kiriha.

Kyo's head dropped between his shoulders. I couldn't help but laugh. Kiriha let out an exasperated sigh, then turned back to me.

"But he's right, you know," she said. "You let things weigh pretty heavily on yourself, and sometimes you need to let go and rest. This is especially true now that you're going to a whole other country where you don't know anyone. You're going to feel anxious sometimes. I bet it'll be the same as when we first got here—we weren't used to being surrounded by humans."

"Yeah, good point," I said.

When I'd first come to Luqvist, I was scared and worried,

but that would have been nothing compared to how Kiriha and Kyo would have felt. It couldn't have been easy for them, surrounded by humans, most of whom didn't like them.

"But I'll be fine," I said. "I'm going to where Usato came from. I'm sure everyone there will be kind to me."

Even Usato himself had said that the rescue team—aside from their rugged appearance—were all good people at heart, so I didn't think I had to worry about that.

"Yeah, it's that attitude that I'm a little worried about," said Kiriha, "but if you say you'll be okay, then I guess you'll be okay."

"Oh, I should probably get going," I said.

It wasn't much longer before the carriage would depart. There was no exact time set, but seeing as the merchant was going to be kind enough to take me, I didn't want to be late.

"Alright then. Good luck, Nack," said Kyo. "Make the most of your time in the Llinger Kingdom."

I laughed.

"We're practically neighbors, so I can always come see you guys when I want to," I said.

"That's true," said Kyo with a chuckle.

He was a bit rowdy and a bit rough around the edges, but Kyo was a good guy—he was always looking out for the people he cared about.

"Don't let Usato influence you too much," said Kiriha. "We

don't want to be bewildered by a complete change in personality the next time we see you."

I laughed again.

"Yeah, I don't think *that's* going to happen."

"Well, I've still got my fingers crossed . . ."

Kiriha's comment worried me a little. In any case, she'd been a huge source of support for me. The food she cooked was delicious, and I felt it was her quiet kindness that saved me on more than a few occasions. It was strange to think that my two best friends in Luqvist were beastkin, but I didn't think that was a bad thing at all.

I took a deep breath and composed myself.

"Kiriha, Kyo," I said. "Thanks so much for everything you did to help me until now! We part ways for now, but I'm sure we'll meet again!"

"If we get some time, we'll come see you in Llinger," said Kiriha.

"Great! Well then, until then!" I said.

And with that, I turned around and walked off. I held my head high and did my best to keep all my sentimental thoughts at bay. I knew that if I turned around now, I'd stop walking and I'd start crying. I'd made up my mind, and I was determined to see my goals to completion, so I kept on walking until my two friends were well out of sight.

"According to the headmistress' message, the merchant carriage should be around here somewhere," I muttered.

I'd left Kiriha and Kyo's home and was now near the gates to exit Luqvist. I looked around in search of the merchant carriage that would take me to Llinger.

"Where is it?"

There were a lot of carriages stopped near the city gates. There were plenty of people, too, but I couldn't tell which of them was my ride.

"I guess I'll just have to ask someone."

I let out a little sigh and mustered up the courage to stop someone passing by. But just as I was about to do so, I caught sight of the city from the gates and stopped in place.

"I'm really leaving today," I uttered as the reality impressed itself upon me.

I looked at the cityscape that had become a part of my everyday life and the busy main street, lively with students. I looked at all of it and felt a feeling of awe wash over me. It had always been such a dark and gloomy place for me, but finally, here and now, it struck me as breathtaking.

"This is where it begins," I said. "This is where my new life starts."

It was my journey to join the rescue team.

"What are you doing, just standing around like that?"

The voice behind me caught me completely by surprise. It

was followed up by a kick in the back.

"Huh?!" I said, lurching forwards, baffled.

I knew that irrational, arrogant voice.

"What are *you* doing, sneaking up on me like that?! What do you want, Mina?!"

My old childhood friend and former bully, Mina, stood looking down at me with her arms crossed.

"Nothing, really," she said. "I was just going for a walk, and then I saw an idiot standing around in the middle of the road. Figured I'd give you a gentle shove."

"Mina . . ."

She hadn't mellowed out in the slightest. Not only had she not learned a thing from our battle, it had only encouraged her to be more of who she was.

"So you're leaving," she said.

"How did you know?"

"Halpha told me."

Why did I suddenly feel betrayed for my kindness? Then again, it wasn't like I'd done him any great favors.

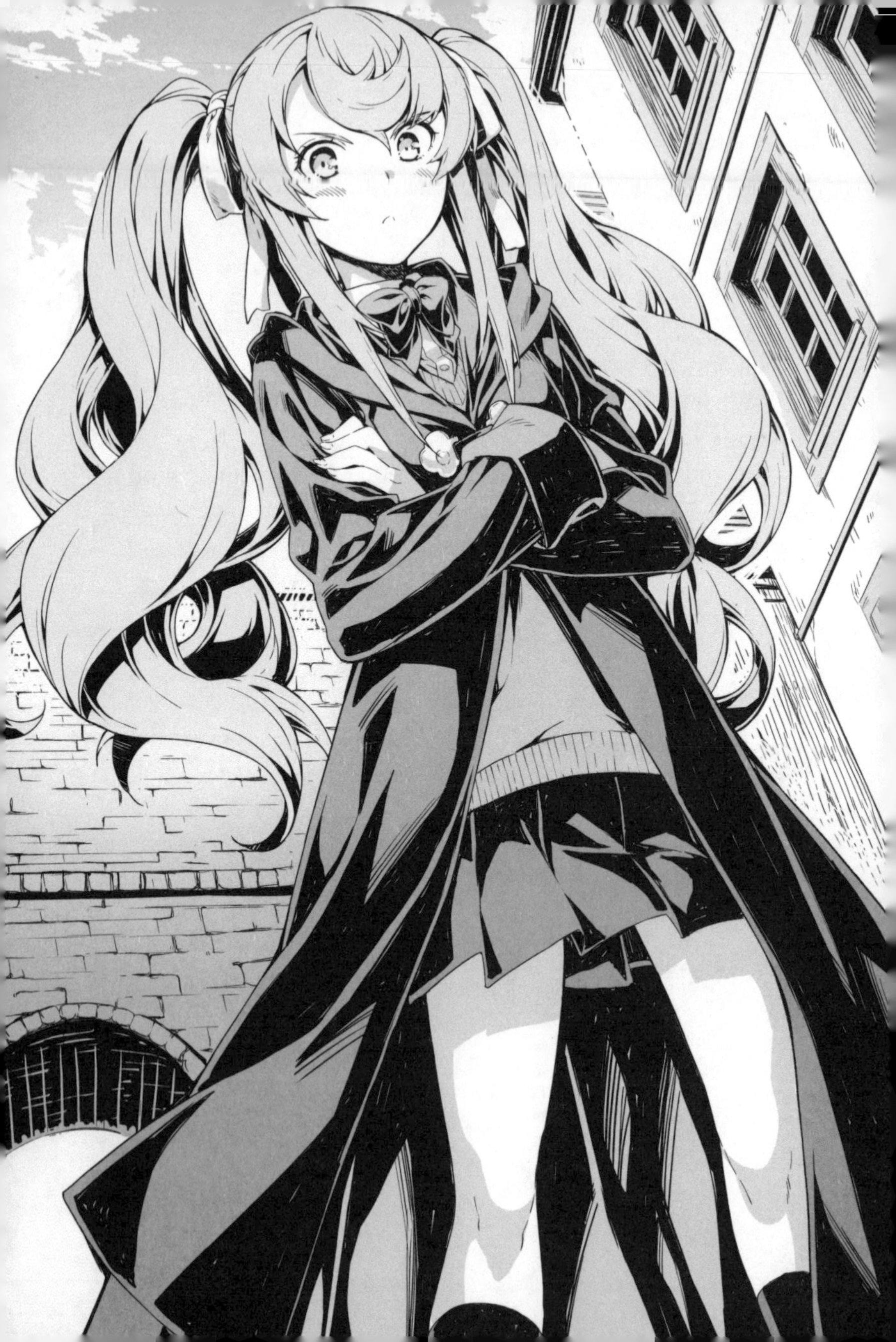

Hang on a second. If Halpha told Mina that I was going to be here, then she's not just out on a casual stroll at all.

"So you're not just out on a walk," I said.

"I am so."

"No, but . . ."

"I'm out on a walk," Mina said stubbornly.

"Yeah, but Halpha . . ."

"How many times do I have to say it?"

"Fine."

She was very intent on maintaining the "out on a walk" excuse. But why was she trying so hard to hide the fact that she was here to see me?

I sighed.

"Look, please don't bother me," I said. "I have to look for the merchant who is going to take me to the Llinger Kingdom."

I waited for Mina to fire back, but I heard only silence.

"Hm?" I murmured.

What's going on? Outside of her initial kick, Mina isn't being herself.

It was weird, but then I noticed that Mina was silently pointing to the left, behind me.

"What are you doing?" I asked.

"The merchant you're looking for is over there," she said.

I looked more closely in the direction that Mina was pointing and noticed a slightly bigger carriage than all the others.

People around were getting ready for departure. Mina was exactly right—that *was* the merchant I was looking for.

"Why did you help me?" I asked.

"I just happened to know it was there. That's all. And then there was you looking all confused . . . and look—after you talked all big to me after our battle, I had to make sure you ended up doing what you said you would. Otherwise, you'd just make me look like an idiot with that promise!"

"Uh, wait. What? Why are you so angry all of a sudden?"

"I'm angry at your stupidity!"

This girl really had her hands full with all the bursts of weird kindness and sudden rage. But this wasn't scary to me anymore—not now that Usato had hardened me to it. One thing was surprising, though.

"So you think of it as a promise," I said.

On the day Usato had left Luqvist, Mina and I had talked. I told her that I was going to Llinger Kingdom, and that I'd wait for her there.

I was surprised that she remembered.

But the moment Mina realized the meaning of what I'd said, she blushed. Or at least, I felt like she did. The reason I wasn't completely sure was because she stood in front of me, expressionless, as she formed burst magic in her palm.

So maybe the redness in her face is just a result of the heat. But even then, it might just be my imagination. Her eyes are growing a touch misty.

"Wait, so you were lying?" she asked.

"N-no..."

Mina's usually aggressive expression fell silent as she walked toward me slowly, her burst magic still in hand. I felt suddenly in a very precarious situation.

"You said all of that, and you don't think of it as a promise?" she asked.

"Erm..."

My instincts screamed at me not to disagree with her. That, and I was also aware that it was my fault for what I'd said.

"N-no, it's not that," I stammered. "That was true. I was serious. I swear it on my sister's name."

I wondered if that last part was going too far. In any case, I backed away slowly, and when I looked up at Mina, she had extinguished her magic and crossed her arms. She looked unimpressed.

"Let me tell you one thing, Nack," she said. "I *hate* lies."

"Huh?"

"I hate being ignored too. And being forgotten. But what I hate most of all is when people go back on what they say."

What is she trying to say?

I was suddenly confused by what felt like something very profound. Mina glared at me.

"After everything you said to me, you better make sure you live up to your words and get stronger."

"Mina," I uttered.

"Those healers for the rescue team? I bet you can't half-ass your way into a position like that. And you must really want it, seeing as you screamed it at the top of your voice in the middle of our fight."

Mina remembered. She remembered what I shouted during our fight. The astonishment in my heart felt suddenly overwhelmed by how impressed I was. Even after everything she had put me through, Mina had, in her own way, accepted the goal that I was reaching for. It made me so happy.

"You threw away your noble title, and now you're leaving Luqvist. If you want it that bad, then I demand that you make it happen. Don't you dare back down on your word. Become a healer for the rescue team. Make that a reality."

Was Mina cheering me on in her own unique and overly aggressive way?

It creeped me out a little to see her attitude change so much, but nonetheless, I was happy about this change inside of her.

Perhaps at this rate, she'll calm her bullying, tormenting thoughts and...

"If you don't become a full-fledged healer, then I can't go all out on you when we fight," Mina stated.

I said nothing. I couldn't speak a word, in fact—Mina's smile and her words were anything but filled with kindness.

Usato, I can't do it! This girl is legitimately crazy! She doesn't even think like an ordinary human does!

"I am going to get even stronger than I am now," said Mina. "I am going to master mana boosting, and I am going to learn to fully control my fireballs. But if I do that and all you are is quick on your feet, then what is even the point?!"

I take back everything I said about being impressed.

I still couldn't speak a word. Mina looked like she was really enjoying herself. In cases like this, it was best just to not show any fear and to accept things head on.

"You just watch then," I said. "I'm going to join the rescue team and become strong enough to stand side by side with Usato. I'm going to stand head and shoulders above my competition."

"Big talk for someone so small. I don't believe it."

Ouch. Hit a guy where it hurts, why don't you?

"But you're the same height as me!" I shot back.

"I'm a girl; it doesn't matter!"

"You don't seem like much of a girl to . . ."

Before I could finish my comeback, Mina's glare silenced me. I really had no idea where the line was for her and how not to cross it. In any case, we'd been talking a while already. I had to make sure I got to the merchant carriage before it left.

"Anyway, thanks for pointing out the merchant carriage for me," I said. "I have to go."

I turned around and made to leave

"Wait right there."

"Hurk!" I grunted as Mina grabbed me by the collar.

I spun back around.

"What's the big idea?!" I asked.

"Here," said Mina.

"Huh?"

Mina had a letter in her hands.

I took it from her, but it puzzled me.

"It's from your sister," stated Mina.

"What? How?"

"It arrived at my place last night, but it's addressed to you."

I turned the envelope over in my hand and saw my name written on the back of it in handwriting much neater and nicer than my own. Was it possible that my parents passed my message on to my sister? Was such a thing even possible?

It hadn't been very long since I sent my letter, but it was enough time for someone to send a reply. I opened the envelope, careful not to rip it, and with shaky hands I took a letter from it. It was written by my sister, whom I hadn't seen in many years.

I am doing well.
I wish you all the best.

It was just two short and concise lines, but her neat script was a touch rushed, as if she had written the letter in a hurry. I could see just how desperate she was to write me a reply. In just two lines, I felt everything she wanted to say.

My sister was in good health, and she was still cheering me on—me, her useless brother who had relinquished his position in the family. I burned her words into my mind, then looked up at Mina, who for some reason had a sulky look on her face.

"Thank you, Mina," I said.

"Don't thank me. I just didn't want your sister's request to go ignored."

"All the same, thank you."

Mina responded with a loud "Hmph" and looked away. I put the letter neatly in with the letter that Usato had given me. I didn't think I would ever hear my sister's voice again, so I never imagined she would ever send me a letter.

Now I truly had zero regrets.

"Okay, now I'm going for real," I said.

"Yeah, you do whatever you want," muttered Mina.

I threw my rucksack on my back and looked at Mina. She still had her arms crossed. She still looked unimpressed. I didn't have anything left to say. I don't know if she did, either, but then I didn't think that either of us needed any kind of dramatic parting words.

She was my childhood friend, my bully, and now my new rival. We'd promised to one day fight again, and though it was weird to think about too deeply, I figured it was all good. I guess the problem was how our relationship would change over time. Still, I was hopeful that things would work out fine. I didn't have any proof of this—just a sense that it would.

We'd know for sure some time in the future, after both of us had grown. Where would I be then? Would I be an exceptional rescue team healer, standing alongside Usato?

Whatever future it was that awaited me, I couldn't wait to meet it.

Without another word, I turned away from Mina and headed for the merchant carriage.

"This is where it all begins," I said.

A life of my own, where nobody tied me down.

I knew that it wasn't going to be easy. It was going to be tougher than anything I'd been through until now, and that reality would be so harsh that sometimes I'd want to cry. But I'd chosen this path for myself, so I would stand up no matter how many times I fell. I would keep on going.

It was with these feelings burning in my chest that I took my first steps toward becoming a member of the rescue team.

The Wrong Way To Use Healing Magic 4   **283**

ONE PEACE BOOKS

The Wrong Way to Use Healing Magic Volume 4
(CHIYUMAHO NO MACHIGATTA TSUKAIKATA -SENJO O KAKERU KAI-HUKUYOIN- Vol. 4)
©KUROKATA 2017
First published in Japan in 2017 by KADOKAWA CORPORATION, Tokyo. English translation rights arranged with KADOKAWA CORPORATION, Tokyo.

ISBN: 978-1-64273-332-7

No part of this may be reproduced or transmitted in any form or by any means, electronic or mechanical, including photocopying, recording, or by storage and retrieval system without the written permission of the publisher. For information contact One Peace Books. Every effort has been made to accurately present the work presented herein. The publisher and authors regret unintentional inaccuracies or omissions, and do not assume responsibility for the accuracy of the translation in this book. Neither the publishers nor the artists and authors of the information presented in herein shall be liable for any loss of profit or any other commercial damages, including but not limited to special, incidental, consequential or other damages.

Written by KUROKATA
Art by KeG
Translated by Hengtee Lim
English Edition Published by One Peace Books 2024

Printed in Canada
1 2 3 4 5 6 7 8 9 10

One Peace Books
43-32 22nd Street STE 204 Long Island City New York 11101